TROPIC

A six-month nursing contract in West Africa will give Kate Mathews just the time she needs to remove any doubts she has about her engagement to David, her childhood sweetheart.

Yet when her new boss, the arrogant Dr Richard Brooks echoes her doubts, why is she suddenly so determined that nothing he says will stop her marriage?

TROPICAL NURSE

BY
MARGARET BARKER

MILLS & BOON LIMITED
London · Sydney · Toronto

First published in Great Britain 1983
by Mills & Boon Limited, 15–16 Brook's Mews,
London W1A 1DR

ISBN 0 263 74233 4

Set in 10 on 11½ pt Linotron Times
03/0383

Photoset by Rowland Phototypesetting Ltd
Bury St Edmunds, Suffolk
Made and printed in Great Britain by
Richard Clay (The Chaucer Press) Ltd
Bungay, Suffolk

CHAPTER ONE

'FASTEN your seat belts. We shall be landing at Ikeja airport in ten minutes.'

The voice over the intercom took Kate by surprise. The last lap of the journey; Nigeria and then over the border into Matala. It was all so exciting! Kate could not believe that she was actually returning to West Africa after all this time. Hastily she pulled a mirror from her bag and ran a comb through her long dark hair. Remembering how hot it would be on the ground, she piled her hair on top of her head. Yes, it would be cooler that way. Now a touch of makeup, but not too much—it would only melt away in the tropical heat. She smiled at her reflection. The new hairstyle accentuated her high cheek-bones and made her look very attractive.

The plane came gently down on the tarmac; the doors were opened and as Kate stepped out she felt as if she were walking into an oven. High above, the afternoon sun beat relentlessly down, and the familiar smells of her tropical childhood assailed her nostrils. Yes, this was the Africa she remembered, but how the airport had changed! Fifteen years ago when she had left it, there had been a small, simple landing strip and a few buildings. Now it was streamlined, shiny and enormous, the whole of it dominated by a control tower which looked like something out of 2001.

The Customs and Immigration hall was crowded as Kate battled her way through, trying desperately to see her case on the conveyor belt. At last she recognised the expensive leather suitcase which her grandmother had insisted on buying for her. Clasping it firmly, she was about to walk away when she found her way barred by the tall figure of a man, holding an almost identical case. Raising her eyes to his face, Kate saw that he was furious.

'I believe you are about to make off with my case,' he thundered, thrusting the other one in her direction. 'This, I think, is yours.'

'Oh, I'm so sorry,' Kate said nervously. 'They are so much alike.'

'I agree, but there is such a thing as reading the labels—that is assuming you *can* read.'

This was more than Kate could take; picking up her case she made off as quickly as possible. It seemed ages before she was finally through Customs and Immigration, and free to walk out of the airport. She was relieved to find a car and an African driver waiting for her, and she urged him to drive off as quickly as possible.

They drove for about five miles to the Nigerian frontier, and crossed over into Matala. The contrast between the two countries was immediately apparent. The Nigerian road from the airport to the frontier had been smooth and wide, but once over the frontier, it was as if the clock had been turned back half a century. The car bumped along a narrow, dusty track. Occasionally Kate saw a woman sitting beside a pile of green oranges, trying to sell them to the passers-by. She remembered, as a child, being surprised to find that oranges in England were not green.

About ten miles from the frontier, the car turned into a gateway marked 'Ikawa Nursing Home', and drove up a short drive, with tall palm trees on either side. The car stopped in front of a long, low, colonial-style building. A verandah ran along the front of the house, from which wide wooden steps led down to the drive. Kate was about to get out of the car when she noticed an airport taxi pulling up behind them. A tall figure climbed out and rushed angrily up to her driver.

'You were supposed to meet me at the airport,' he bellowed. 'Why on earth did you drive off without me?'

Kate recognised the man she had annoyed at the airport. She shrank back in her seat, but he noticed her.

'Ah, it's you again. You seem to enjoy making life difficult for me,' he said, as he opened her door. 'Allow me to introduce myself; I'm Dr Brooks, and you I presume are the new nurse.'

'Yes, I'm Kate Mathews,' said Kate quietly as she got out of the car.

The driver came forward, still apologising.

'Nobody tell me to bring two people from the airport. Madam she say she in plenty big hurry, so I come quick.'

'That's OK, Buba. It's not your fault,' said Dr Brooks, 'Perhaps you could take Nurse Mathews along to meet Dr Clark.'

With that he hurried up the steps and disappeared into the house.

What an odious man, thought Kate. I hope I don't have to see too much of him while I'm here. She followed Buba along a corridor to a door on which the name 'Dr Clark' was printed in bold letters. Buba tapped lightly on the door and left Kate when an answer came from inside. She went in and found an attractive man, with greying hair, sitting at a desk. He smiled as she entered, and stood up to welcome her.

'Hello, you must be Kate Mathews. We were expecting you—and Dr Brooks too. Did you travel from the airport with him?'

'Er, well not exactly. The driver set off without him, and he had to take a taxi.'

'Oh dear, he won't like that. He hates inefficiency. I shall have to try and smooth things out when I see him. He's going to be in charge here while I'm in the UK for six months.'

Kate's heart sank.

'I'm lucky to find someone of his calibre,' continued Dr Clark. 'He was medical registrar at Kyruba Hospital, before he went home on leave. Well now, let's talk about you. Do sit down and make yourself comfortable. You must be exhausted after your long journey.'

'Well no, not really. I enjoyed most of it. It's nice to be back in West Africa.'

'Back? I thought this was your first assignment over here.'

'Oh yes, the first time I've nursed here, but I was actually born out here, and I lived here until I was six.'

'Were you really! Good heavens, I must have known your parents. I've been out here twenty years. Let me see—Mathews—why of course! Agriculture and Fisheries Officer. You lived in that lovely house near the Ogiwa Dam.'

Kate nodded happily. 'It was marvellous living there. I had such a happy time when I was a child, and then . . .' Her voice trailed off, and Dr Clark spoke quickly,

'Yes, I was sorry to hear about your father's death. In actual fact he came to me for an examination, because of his recurrent hepatitis. I advised him to go back to the UK as soon as possible. It was carcinoma of the liver, wasn't it?'

'Yes; there was nothing anyone could do. My mother took it very badly.'

'I imagine she would. You know, I didn't connect you

with the Mathews' family when the agency sent me your details. Let me see now . . .' He rustled through his papers. 'I see you live in Yorkshire now, so you must have moved from London.'

'Yes, we went to live with my grandparents soon after Daddy died. Mummy found she just couldn't cope on her own.'

'I see,' Dr Clark looked extremely thoughtful. There was a short pause, then he continued.

'Actually, I met your mother in London some weeks after your father's death—quite by chance, of course,' he added quickly. 'I remember she said she was planning to move to the country somewhere . . . Well, what a coincidence! June Mathews' daughter! Still, I might have known it. A good-looking girl like you.'

He stopped, looking slightly embarrassed. 'But surely your mother told you we were old friends?'

'Well actually I haven't seen her since I decided to come out here. She's on a touring holiday in America with her sister. I sent a letter to one of the hotels where they planned to stay, but I haven't had a reply yet.'

'Quite a surprise for her I should think. Will she mind?'

'I hope not! But still, I am twenty-one.'

'Positively ancient!' he laughed. 'How do you find Matala after all these years?'

'Nothing seems to have changed. The roads are still as bad as ever!'

'Ah yes. There's never any money to spend on improvements. The government keeps changing, and we stagger on from one crisis to another. We're not an oil-rich country like Nigeria. There is real poverty in the town of Kyruba and in the small villages. Life is very much as it was fifty years ago. Many of the young

Matalans go to live in Nigeria, hoping to make their fortune, very few succeed of course. Well now, let's see if we can find some tea.'

They went out of the office and along a corridor to a verandah at the back of the house, where two people were sitting at a long, low table. One was a small blonde nurse, who was introduced as Julie Smith. The other was the daunting figure of Dr Brooks. He stood up and shook hands with Dr Clark, who welcomed him warmly.

'Richard, my dear chap, how marvellous to see you. Sorry about the mix-up at the airport. Buba is a good driver, but he's never very sure of his instructions. Still you're here now, which is all that matters. I believe you've met Kate Mathews already.'

Dr Brooks smiled briefly,

'Yes, you could say that. How do you do, Nurse Mathews,' he continued stiffly, whilst his eyes seemed to pierce through her.

'I hope you've recovered from your journey, Dr Brooks,' murmured Kate politely.'

There was something about his eyes that unnerved her. He looked amused at her confusion. She sat down hurriedly in the nearest chair, and to add to her distress he sauntered over and sat next to her, without taking his eyes from her face.

'So what brings a beautiful young nurse like you to this part of the world?' he asked, in a supercilious voice.

'I used to live in Matala when I was a child, and I wanted to see the country again.' Kate had regained her composure.

'Oh, I see. A nostalgic trip down memory lane.' He was smiling now, but his eyes were hard, steely grey and cold. Kate found him difficult to understand. Was he mocking her?

'In a way, I suppose,' she answered lamely.

At that moment the steward arrived and started to serve tea. Kate was thankful for the interruption.

'Isn't it amazing,' said Dr Clark,' I used to know Kate's family. They lived about ten miles from here.'

He turned to Kate. 'The people who live in your old house now are great friends of mine—John Miller and his family—he's the medical consultant at Kyruba Hospital. You must meet them while you're out here. I wish I could show you around myself, but I'm booked on the plane for tomorrow, and I've several engagements in London next week.'

'Is this business or pleasure?' asked Kate.

'Both—I need a holiday and I've got some problems on my estate in Scotland. One day soon I plan to retire there—hang up my stethoscope and take up fishing. I've been drifting along out here for far too long. My wife died when I was twenty-eight—we'd only been married two years, and I came out here to forget. I should have gone home long since. Still I've enjoyed my time out here. Now you must excuse me if I dash along. There's such a lot to be finished before I leave. Richard, can you spare me a few minutes in the office. There are a number of things we must sort out. Perhaps we can all meet later for a drink. Julie, you'll look after Kate, won't you.'

'I most certainly will,' said Julie. 'Come on, I'll show you to your room. I expect you'd like a shower. Phew! I'll never get used to this heat. Good thing you've lived out here. Were you born in Matala?'.

'No I was actually born across the border in Nigeria. The maternity facilities were somewhat primitive in Matala in those days.'

'Still are! Kyruba Hospital has improved, but most

Europeans still go to Nigeria or come here, if they can afford us!'

Kate followed Julie along a corridor and out into the garden at the back of the building. The fragrance of frangipani and tropical roses filled the air, and the sun was pleasantly warm. They went on to a verandah and in through the open french windows of Kate's room. It was spotlessly clean, and the woodwork of the floor and furniture gleamed with polish. At the back of the room was a door, leading to a tiny shower room. A bowl of roses had been placed on the dressing table.

'How charming it all looks,' said Kate. 'Do all the nurses have a room like this?'

'There are only the two of us,' said Julie. 'Yes I've got a room like this too.'

'Only two nurses!' said Kate. 'But how on earth do you cope?'

'Oh it's easy. We've only got six patients in at the moment. Our maximum is ten. Well, I'll leave you to unpack. Join me for a drink when you've finished.'

Kate showered, and changed into a cool cotton dress. The peace of the little room enveloped her as she started to unpack. She was about to put David's photograph on the dressing-table when something stopped her. Give yourself a chance, she told herself. Forget home and family for a while. But that was easier said than done. David's handsome face stared out at her from the photograph. She remembered their last evening together, when David had produced a beautiful diamond engagement ring. She had hesitated before trying it on, but David had insisted.

'It belonged to my grandmother,' he told her, 'I want you to have it before you go away.'

'Oh, but I couldn't possibly!' Kate had protested. 'It's

much too valuable. It might get lost or stolen when I'm in Africa.'

But David had insisted she try it on, and it had been too big. Why had she felt relieved? She had firmly turned down the suggestion that it should be made smaller.

'No,' Kate had protested. 'Please don't spoil it. Leave it exactly as it is, but keep it here in England. I can have a clip put on it when I get back.'

David had been puzzled and a little hurt. Kate had tried to analyse her own feelings. Why had she rejected the ring? Was it because it made everything so final? Was it because she was being pushed along once again? Perhaps she resented the fact that David had never actually asked her to marry him. It had always been taken for granted that she would. As a small child she had hero-worshipped him. Because he was three years older than her, he had treated her as a tiresome younger sister at first. David's parents had befriended her newly-widowed mother, and Kate and David had spent much of their childhood together. As they grew older, their friendship blossomed into romance, and everyone assumed they would marry.

She put the photograph into a drawer and closed it guiltily. After all, she had six months to sort out her feelings—six months of freedom. As soon as she had seen the advertisement in the paper, she had known that was what she wanted to do—escape.

'*SRN required immediately for six months in West African nursing home.*' It had leapt out at her from the page, and before she knew where she was, she was on the phone to the nursing agency.

Looking out across the garden, Kate saw that Dr Brooks and Julie were already on the verandah. She left her room and went over to join them. Dr Brooks was poring intently over a file of papers, but Julie turned to greet her.

'Well there you are! I thought you were never coming.'

Dr Brooks merely nodded in her direction and continued reading his notes. Kate sat down next to Julie.

'What do you want to drink?' she asked.

'Er . . . gin and tonic, I think,' said Kate hesitantly.

'What do you usually have?' asked Julie.

'Well actually I don't drink much,' said Kate defensively.

'Oh, you'll soon learn out here, won't she Dr Brooks?'

Dr Brooks looked annoyed at this further interruption and ignored them.

'Musa!' called Julie to the steward. 'Another gin and tonic please.'

Musa appeared with Kate's drink, and placed it on the table in front of her. Julie was apparently delighted to have someone to talk to. She asked endless questions about England, and what was happening at the moment. Then suddenly she said,

'Did you enjoy living in Matala when you were a child?'

'Oh, very much,' Kate replied, and she became aware that Dr Brooks was now listening. He lazily turned his head towards her and said,

'So you decided to take a working holiday back in the tropics.' His cold grey eyes seemed to be weighing her up. 'Or is there some other reason?'

Kate was momentarily taken aback. Was he trying to be rude, or was this just his normal manner?

'I simply wanted to see Matala again,' she said, feeling annoyed that she should have to be so defensive about it.

'And what did mummy and daddy think about this?' he continued relentlessly.

'My father is dead, and my mother always respects my independence. This is something I must do before I get married.'

'Ah yes—the young girls' dream to get married and settle down.'

'Not at all,' said Kate angrily.

'I do beg your pardon,' he said, with heavy sarcasm. 'I naturally assumed that you were just another young nurse in search of a husband.'

'Then you were wrong. I happen to enjoy my work, and I'm hoping to gain some experience of tropical nursing.'

'Not much tropical nursing here,' said Julie. 'Most of our patients are rich Europeans, who live in air-conditioned houses. If you want to see real tropical nursing, you'll have to go to Kyruba hospital.'

At that moment Dr Clark appeared.

'Sorry I'm late. I've been trying to finish my paper-work. I think I've left everything organised for you.'

He accepted his drink. 'Thank you, Musa.' He turned to Kate. 'When does your mother get back from America? I thought I might pop in on my way up to Scotland, and tell her you're OK.'

'Oh she'd like that. She gets back next week some-time.'

'Well that's settled then. Come on, Richard, let's start the evening round. No need for you to come just yet, Julie—finish your drink. Tomorrow you can all start the new routine without me. Don't be too hard on them, Richard,' he laughed.

The two men went off in the direction of the medical wing.

'Do you like our new MD?' asked Julie, when the men had gone.

'I think he's arrogant and conceited,' said Kate, emphatically.

'Oh, but he's so good-looking when he smiles. Tall, dark and handsome! Mm! Pity he's married. It would have been nice to have some new talent around the place. At least, I think he is. I went to his room to tell him drinks were served, and there was a woman's photograph on his desk. I asked him if it was his wife and he said "What do you think?"'

'Quite frankly, I couldn't care less,' said Kate. 'For one thing I don't like him and for another I'm engaged already.'

'Oh really? That's nice for you. When's the great day?'

'Oh, not for ages yet,' said Kate.

Julie stood up. 'Well, must away, duty calls. No need for you to come round tonight. We'll show you the ropes tomorrow.'

Kate sat very still after Julie had gone, listening to the evening sounds. It was quiet except for the steady clicking of the insects out in the garden. Suddenly she heard a strange noise at the end of the verandah. A land crab was clambering along the wooden floor, making towards the house. Kate took it back into the garden, and stayed for a few minutes soaking up the peace of the twilight. A couple of lizards dashed across her path, their long tails wriggling furiously, and the crimson of their heads shining in the last rays of the setting sun. All too soon the brief twilight ended and darkness fell. The night sounds of Africa enveloped her, and Kate felt that she was really at home again. She was glad to be back in Matala, but a little apprehensive of the new situation.

Julie seemed pleasant enough, and Dr Clark was charming, but the less she saw of Richard Brooks the better!

CHAPTER TWO

KATE woke next morning when Musa brought in her tea-tray. What a civilised way to start the day! Much better than being awakened by the ringing of a noisy bell in the nurses' home. She looked at her watch—only seven o'clock and the sun was already warm. Musa opened the french windows and disappeared as quietly as he had arrived. Kate sat up and started to drink her tea. There was a tap on the door and Julie came in, draped in a flowery housecoat.

'Wakey, wakey! Rise and shine. Breakfast at seven-thirty. I've brought your uniform. Anything else you need?'

'No, I seem to have everything, thank you.'

'OK, I'll see you at breakfast on the verandah.'

When Julie had gone, Kate dressed in the white dress and cap. She examined her reflection in the mirror, and saw that the tropical uniform looked good on her.

When she arrived at the breakfast table, she was aware that Dr Brooks was looking at her in an appraising way.

'Good morning,' he said. 'Did you sleep well?'

'Like a log after I'd turned off the air-conditioning and fixed the mosquito net.'

'Oh, give me air-conditioning every time. Still I suppose it's what you get used to. Did you have mosquito nets when you were a child?' he continued amicably.

'Yes, we were very primitive at Ogiwa House,' laughed Kate. He's really rather nice when he gets off his

18

high horse, she thought, as she helped herself to toast
and coffee.

'I always think this is the best part of the day,' said
Julie. 'Before it gets too hot.'

'It's like England on a good summer day,' Dr Brooks
was really smiling, not just with his mouth, but his eyes
had a warm look too as he turned to Kate. 'Nurse Smith
tells me you are engaged to be married. Congratulations! When's the big event?'

'Oh, nothing's settled yet. My fiancé has to finish his
year as a house surgeon, and then he's going to join his
father in the family practice.'

'Sounds a nice cushy number. A good catch I should
say.' Dr Brooks smiled his mocking smile.

Kate was furious! How dare he be so rude! She
finished her breakfast in stony silence. Julie made several attempts at conversation, but found herself ignored.
Dr Brooks broke the silence eventually.

'I've got to go to Kyruba hospital when we've done the
morning round. Would you like to come with me, Nurse
Mathews?'

Kate was completely taken aback. Was this another
attempt at friendship? If so, would he rebuff her as soon
as she was off her guard?

'Yes, I would like to see Kyruba again,' she said
cautiously.

'Fine, will you take charge, Julie? You can always ring
me at the hospital if you need me, but I don't foresee any
problems today.'

'Don't worry—I shall be OK,' said Julie.

'Of course you will.' Dr Brooks gave Julie one of his
charming smiles. 'Dr Clark tells me you're extremely
capable.'

He certainly knows how to handle people, thought

Kate, as she made a decision to remain coolly profess-ional towards him. She would not allow him to annoy her again.

When breakfast was over they set off to do the morn-ing round. They went first to the reception area where an African male nurse was sitting by the switchboard.

'Anything to report, Joseph?' asked Dr Brooks.

'No sir, it's been a very quiet night.'

'Fine. You can go off duty now.'

They walked along the corridor and went into the first door. A pleasant looking young woman was sitting up in bed, reading.

'Good morning, Mrs Benson,' said Dr Brooks. 'How are we today?'

'We're both very well, Doctor.' Mrs Benson patted the large lump under the bedclothes, happily. 'He's been kicking like mad in the night.'

'Oh, so it's a he, is it?' said Dr Brooks, 'Let's have a listen.'

He palpated the abdomen and listened to the baby's heart.

'Very much alive and well. Won't be long now.'

'I hope not. My husband's getting very lonely without me.'

'Oh, we'll have you home in no time at all,' Dr Brooks assured her.

As they moved on to the next room, Dr Brooks told Kate that Mrs Benson had high blood pressure, and at eight months pregnant they were taking no chances.

They went into the next room, where they found a tall, slim lady, sitting by the open windows, manicuring her nails.

'Oh, Doctor, I'm so glad you've come. I haven't slept a wink all night, and that dreadful man on night duty wouldn't give me anything to help me sleep. I told him to call you, but he said it wasn't necessary. Quite frankly, I don't know what I'm paying you for.'

'But I gave you a sleeping pill before I went off duty,' said Julie.

'Yes, and it didn't work. I just can't go on like this,' her voice rose hysterically.

'There now, don't worry, Mrs Marshall,' said Dr Brooks, soothingly. 'We'll see what we can do tonight.' He favoured her with his most charming smile, and she melted visibly.

Quite a ladies' man, thought Kate. He turns the charm on like water from the tap.

'Phew!' said Julie, when they were safely outside. 'Good thing they're not all like that! There's nothing wrong with her. She's supposed to be suffering from nervous exhaustion, but she just comes in here every so often for a rest cure. She treats me like a chamber-maid. Still she can afford it so I suppose we must pamper her.'

The third patient was suffering from psoriasis. Sitting in his chair, with flakes of skin falling everywhere, he was a pathetic sight, but he smiled bravely when they went in.

'Hello, Mr Brown, had a good night?'

'Can't grumble, Doctor. Went out like a light after I'd taken my pill. Still losing my skin, though, I look like a snake, don't I!'

'I'll be along soon to put your ointment on,' said Julie. 'I wish everyone was as cheerful as you.'

They continued on their round. The fourth patient was a man who had recently suffered a mild heart attack. The fifth room housed a post-operative appendix case, and in the sixth room was their only African patient. Chief Ladipo was a very large jolly man, confined to bed with a fractured femur, suffered in a car crash. He laughed and joked with them, and insisted that they must all visit him at his palace when he was better.

Dr Clark came down the corridor, as they were finishing their round. He was dressed in a dark suit, ready for his journey.

'Goodbye, everybody. Don't work too hard.'

'Give my love to Mummy, if you see her,' said Kate.

'But of course I will, Kate. Richard, I hear you're going down to Kyruba today. Tell John Miller I'm still considering his proposition,' he said mysteriously. 'I'll let him know soon what I've decided. Must go—see you all in six months.'

Kate felt a slight feeling of panic as the friendly figure went off to the waiting car. The prospect of a whole day with Dr Richard Brooks was rather unnerving. As if reading her thoughts, he said,

'Time to be moving off. Nurse Mathews, can you be ready in ten minutes?'

'Why of course, whenever you say.' Kate was going to be efficiency itself.

In exactly ten minutes they were driving down the bumpy track which led to Kyruba. Gradually the scenery became familiar to Kate. She saw the outline of trees which surrounded the Ogiwa Dam, where she had lived as a child.

'Do you think we could drive over to have a look at my old home, Dr Brooks?' she asked hesitantly.

'We can do better than that. I'm going to see John Miller at the hospital. He's always inviting me to go and have a look at his place—today we'll call in on our way back. Now do stop calling me Dr Brooks, my name's Richard when we're off-duty. I presume you don't mind if I call you Kate?'

'Not at all.'

Kate studied the strong, handsome profile as he drove the Land Rover skilfully along the difficult road. He took his eyes briefly from the road, and Kate was annoyed that he caught her studying him. He smiled when he saw her embarrassment and continued to concentrate on his driving. Kate kept her eyes on the road. Soon they were driving through the outskirts of Kyruba. She had not really noticed the squalor and poverty as a child. It was difficult to realise that they were in the twentieth century. Richard drove down to the sea and along the main marina. Palm trees flanked the edge of the road; this was the part the tourists saw, when the cruise ships tied up in the harbour. They arrived at the hospital, which was a solid-looking building, built during the 1930s. Some structural improvements had been made recently, otherwise it remained unchanged.

'Well, you said you wanted to see some tropical nursing, so here it is,' said Richard. He parked the Land Rover, and they went in through the main entrance.

'We'll see John Miller first of all, then I'll find someone to take you round the hospital.'

'Oh, yes, I'd like that,' said Kate, enthusiastically.

'I thought you might.' He smiled down at her, and Kate found herself warming towards him, in spite of herself. They stopped in front of a door marked 'Medical Consultant'.

'Let's hope he's in,' said Richard. They were in luck, and soon found themselves in John Miller's office. A tall, distinguished-looking man in his late thirties welcomed them warmly.

'Richard—how marvellous to see you. Have you had a good leave?'

'Splendid, thank you, John. I'd like you to meet Kate

Mathews. She's come out to nurse at Ikawa for six months. By the most amazing coincidence, she used to live in your house when she was a child.'

'I'm delighted to meet you, Kate. You must come out and see the house. My wife would love to meet you—what are you doing for lunch, Richard? Are you free to come home with me?'

'That's extremely kind of you John. We should be very happy to join you, wouldn't we Kate?' She nodded happily, and Dr Miller smiled.

'You see, it only needed a pretty girl to make you accept my invitation. I'll give Helen a ring and tell her to expect us. Now, would you like to look round the hospital, Kate, while Richard and I talk business?'

'Why yes, if that's convenient.'

'But of course.' He pressed a bell on his desk, and an attractive African girl came in.

'Anna, would you arrange for someone to escort Nurse Mathews round the hospital.'

'Certainly sir. I'll take her myself, if you don't need me.' She gave them a broad smile, displaying perfect white teeth.

The next hour was fascinating for Kate. She saw medical cases which she had only read about in her text books. It was far more stimulating than the round of the nursing home which she had made earlier that morning. Kate was full of praise for the work she had seen when she arrived back at Dr Miller's office. He was impressed by her enthusiasm.

'I'm so glad you found your visit interesting,' he said. 'Perhaps you'd like to come and work here when your contract at Ikawa is finished. What do you think?'

'Well I'd love to, but . . . er . . . I'm not sure what I shall be doing in six months time.'

'What she means is that she's getting married,' Richard explained.

'Well, congratulations!' said Dr Miller. 'I hope you'll be very happy, my dear. Pity we can't keep you out here, though, especially now that Richard may be coming onto the permanent staff.'

'I don't think we should discuss it, until it's all settled,' said Richard quickly, 'It still depends on James Clark's decision.'

'Of course, but I think we can be fairly hopeful,' Dr Miller smiled at Kate. 'Now let me introduce you to another member of our medical team. Kate, this is Mike Gregson; he took over from Richard as medical registrar.'

A tall fair-haired man with a friendly smile came across the room from the desk where he had been working. He shook hands with Kate.

'I'm delighted to meet you, Kate. I hope we shall see more of you while you're out here.' Kate warmed to his infectious grin and laughing eyes.

Dr Miller looked at his watch. 'Come along folks, time for lunch. I'm leaving you in charge, Mike. If you need me give me a ring. Otherwise I plan to take a very long lunch hour.'

Richard and Kate drove off in the Land Rover, following Dr Miller. Richard was silent as he drove through the town, then suddenly he said,

'I think I should warn you, Kate, that Mike Gregson is a terrible Casanova; he chases all the nurses.'

'Oh really? Well I'm perfectly capable of looking after myself, but thanks for the warning anyway,' she said coolly.

They drove on in silence through the outskirts of the town. The road became a long, bumpy track as they

approached Ogiwa House, and then at last they drove
through a wide gateway and round a gravel drive. The
house was a two-storey building, made of stone. It
looked out across a large garden to a magnificent view of
the Ogiwa dam. It was quite breathtaking. Kate got out
of the car and walked towards the house. Dr Miller had
already arrived, and was standing on the steps with his
wife. They came to meet her.

'Welcome to Ogiwa House,' said Dr Miller. 'This is
my wife Helen.'

Helen was a pretty young woman with long, fair hair
and an attractive smile.

She greeted Kate warmly, and the two women went
into the house, leaving the men on the verandah, where
a white-uniformed steward was serving drinks.

Helen took Kate over the house, and Kate was thrilled
to find that very little had changed since she was there.

'It's all so lovely,' she said, when they joined the men
on the verandah. 'I simply can't believe I'm here again.
It's like a dream.'

Helen brought the children out to meet them. There
was Phillip, aged four and Stephanie aged two. They
played happily together while the grown-ups had their
drink. Lunch was served in a large dining-room, overlooking the garden. Afterwards, while the children were
asleep, they went down to the edge of the dam and
sat in the shade of the palm trees. It was very peaceful; the water shone like a mirror in the hot afternoon
sun.

'You're very lucky to have a place like this,' said
Richard.

'I know. I never want to go back to the hospital, once I
get out here.' Dr Miller said. 'Still, I must drag myself
away once more. Can't leave all the work to Mike.

You'll let me know what Dr Clark's decision is as soon as you can, won't you?'

'Yes, of course,' said Richard.

Kate found herself wondering what this mysterious decision was. If Richard's contract at Ikawa was six months, like her own, how did Dr Clark need to give a decision on Richard's return to Kyruba hospital? Anyway it didn't concern her, so she tried to stop thinking about it.

'I must be off now,' Dr Miller was saying, 'but do stay and have some tea with Helen.'

They sat on the verandah, drinking tea and talking until the sun was low in the sky. Reluctantly they took their leave of their charming hostess, and the children, and drove off towards Ikawa. The sun was setting as they reached the hill, above the nursing home. The last rays lit up the valley, in a multitude of bright colours.

'How absolutely beautiful,' Kate breathed.

Richard drove to the edge of the hill, and stopped the Land Rover. They admired the view in silence for a few minutes. The twilight was ending but still they remained. Kate glanced shyly at Richard, and found that he was looking at her, with an expression which she could not understand. She looked into his eyes, and saw nothing but tenderness.

Suddenly he reached towards her and took her in his arms. Breathlessly she waited, unable to understand this unknown man, whose body was throbbing next to hers. Then his mouth came down firmly on hers, crushing her lips. Her body relaxed and, in spite of herself, she found herself responding.

She melted in his warm embrace, feeling soft and pliable; she no longer belonged to herself, but to this strong insistent man who was trying to possess her.

Dimly, from afar, she was aware that he had released his hold of her and was looking at her fondly.

His hand touched her cheek. 'You remind me of someone I used to know,' he murmured softly.

'Was this before or after you were married?' asked Kate.

His attitude changed suddenly. 'I don't think that has anything to do with you,' he said coldly. He sat back in his seat and started up the engine.

They drove to the nursing home in complete silence. Julie was waiting for them when they got back.

'Well, I hope you enjoyed your day out,' she said.

'We did indeed, Julie.' Richard flashed her one of his charming smiles. 'I hope you didn't have too much work.'

'No, I coped easily. This place runs itself. Still, I could do with a shower before supper. Can you do the evening round, Kate?'

'Of course she will,' said Richard. 'Come on, Kate, let's get some work done.' He was his usual efficient self again.

They went round the patients together, listening to the problems and dispensing the evening medication. When they had finished, Kate went to her room for a shower. She changed into a cool dress and went out on to the verandah. Musa was serving drinks to Julie and Richard. It was just like the evening before, except Kate found herself intrigued by Richard. He seemed to focus all his attention on Julie. They laughed and joked together, and Kate felt herself excluded. Suddenly Richard said,

'You're very quiet tonight, Kate. I hope our little outing hasn't tired you too much.'

'Not at all,' said Kate. 'I was admiring the sunset.'

'Yes it is beautiful again,' he said. 'Have you enjoyed your first day back in Matala?'

'Most of it,' said Kate coolly. She stood up. 'I think I'll go to my room. I've got to write a letter.'

'Ah yes, mustn't forget the faithful fiancé back home,' he said in a mocking voice.

'Goodnight,' said Kate quietly, and went across to her room.

'Dear David,' she wrote, and then started again on another sheet.

'My darling David, I am missing you terribly . . .'

Well it was true, wasn't it?

She screwed up the paper and threw it into the waste-bin.

I'll write it tomorrow, she promised herself.

CHAPTER THREE

THE day started sooner than Kate had anticipated. She was awakened by the ringing of her bedside phone at six o'clock. Sleepily she answered it.

'Kate, can you come along to Mrs Benson's room? She's had a slight haemorrhage.'

'Yes, of course,' Kate was immediately awake. 'I'll come at once.'

She found Richard waiting for her outside Mrs Benson's room.

'No need to worry unduly,' he said. 'The bleeding's stopped, but she's rather frightened. I'd like you to stay with her for a while. Take her pulse and blood pressure every half hour, and ring me if you're worried. I didn't want to waken Julie, after her long day yesterday. Do you think you can cope?'

'Of course.' Kate was brisk and efficient, as she turned away from Richard and went into the room.

He followed her in and watched as she took Mrs Benson's blood pressure.

'I'm so glad you're here, Nurse,' said Mrs Benson, weakly. 'I was feeling so scared. Do you think the baby's all right?'

'Yes, of course,' said Richard. 'We've listened to his heartbeat, and he's very much alive. All you've got to do now is lie back and let Nurse take care of you. I'll see you in a little while.'

Kate stayed with Mrs Benson until Julie and Richard

arrived about eight o'clock. Richard examined her and
was pleased with her condition.

'No need to worry,' he said. 'But I think we'd better
keep an eye on you. One of the nurses will come on duty
tonight, to make sure you behave yourself.'

When they were safely outside the door, Richard
turned to Kate and said,

'Perhaps you would take the first duty tonight, Kate.
Go off-duty at lunch-time, and sleep this afternoon. We
can't take any chances at this stage. You have had some
midwifery experience, I presume?'

'Three months during my general training,' said Kate.

Richard frowned. 'Not much . . . you'd better call
Julie if you're the least bit worried. What sort of experience have you had, Julie?'

'Oh, I'm a fully qualified midwife,' said Julie.

'Well, that's a relief.' Richard smiled at her. 'It's good
to have some experienced staff around. I can't run the
place with juniors.'

He walked quickly away, leaving Kate feeling totally
incompetent.

The morning passed uneventfully. Kate found herself
looking forward to an afternoon siesta. After lunch she
went to her room and had a shower. She lay on her bed
and tried to sleep. At first she found her brain was too
active, but gradually she found herself lulled by the
drone of the insects in the garden. When she awoke, the
air was cooler. She dressed and went to the dining-room
for an early supper, by herself. Julie was finishing her
day-report when Kate arrived on duty.

'Ah there you are. Did you manage to sleep?'

'Yes thanks. How's Mrs Benson?'

'She seems OK. No further bleeding today. You'd
better take her pulse and blood pressure every hour, and

call me if you're worried. It would be best if she could go to full term, but if there are going to be any complications we shall have to induce the baby.'

Julie gathered her things from the desk.

'By the way, I told Joseph not to come in. You'll have nothing to do once the patients are asleep. Goodnight.'

Kate spent the next half-hour settling the patients, and then sat down at the desk by the switchboard, in the main hall. It was very quiet. About midnight the swing doors opened and Richard came in.

'Hello there, everything all right?'

Kate found her pulse was racing. She hadn't expected to see him.

'Nothing to report, Doctor,' she answered efficiently.

'Oh come now,' he laughed. 'Is that all you've got to say to me? How about a cup of coffee then?'

Kate smiled. 'I think a junior nurse can just about manage that.'

'I'm sorry. I didn't mean to be rude to you this morning. I had simply expected that you would have done your midwifery training already.'

'Give me a chance,' said Kate. 'I only got my SRN two months ago. I'm only twenty-one. There's plenty of time.'

'Not if you're going to be married soon. Anyway, about that coffee . . .'

They went into the small kitchen and Kate put the coffee on. Richard lowered himself into the only armchair, and Kate hovered nervously by the stove.

'Come over here, for heaven's sake. It's not going to boil over.'

He reached out a hand and pulled her down on to the arm of his chair. 'It's not often I have a pretty girl all to myself, in the middle of the night.'

He brushed his lips against her cheek, and gave her waist a squeeze. She found the same response which had occurred before, but this time it was stronger. Her whole body was yearning to be at one with his. To her dismay she found herself trembling. Apparently Richard had noticed too.

'My dear child, whatever is the matter? You can't possibly be cold.'

'It's the air-conditioning. I never did like it.' Kate jumped up and went over to the stove. 'How do you like your coffee, Richard?'

'Black, please.' He was studying her carefully. 'I really think you're frightened of me,' he laughed.

'No I'm not,' said Kate, 'I just find your constant change of mood difficult to take.'

'Ah, you must learn to tell the difference between my professional and my private self. This morning I was totally preoccupied with the welfare of my patients. Now I'm off-duty.'

Kate looked at the handsome figure reclining in the chair, and she found her heart beating faster, in spite of herself. She perched on the edge of the table, and sipped her coffee.

'You make delicious coffee, Kate,' Richard said, after a few moments had passed.

Kate smiled. 'I'm glad there's a something I can do well.'

'Oh come on, you're going to make an excellent nurse, and you know it. That is if you stick at it long enough. You're not seriously going to bury yourself away in a country practice are you?'

Kate stiffened. 'I'm not going to bury myself any-where. I shall be helping my fiancé and his father. General practice can be very interesting.'

'General dogsbody, that's what you'll be, if you're not careful. Still, if that's what you want, who am I to try and stop you. But it does seem a terrible waste of talent.'

'So what do you think I should do?' Kate asked, with a calmness which she didn't feel.

'Well, at least give yourself time to live a little before you settle down. How old is your fiancé?'

'Twenty-four.'

'There you are you see; you're just a couple of children. I didn't get married until I was twenty-eight.'

'And how old was your wife?'

'My wife?' Richard looked startled. 'Er . . . I can't remember . . . certainly she was older than you.' He stood up. 'I must get some sleep.'

He went to the door; suddenly he turned back, and put his hand on her arm.

'Kate, there's something I must tell you, about my wife . . .'

He was pale and his voice shook with emotion.

'Richard, whatever is the matter?' said Kate. 'Sit down for heaven's sake.'

As she spoke they heard a car screech to a halt outside in the drive.

They ran out through the front entrance, and saw a tall blond man getting out of a station-wagon. He ran up the steps.

'Help me quickly,' he cried. 'My wife's just had a baby, and I'm terribly worried about it. I've brought them both.'

Richard and Kate went down to the car. A young woman was lying on the back seat, clutching a tiny bundle. Richard leaned inside the car.

'We're going to take you inside,' he said. 'Kate, you take the baby.'

He handed her the tiny child, which was beginning to cry feebly, then carried the mother into the reception area, where he laid her on a couch.

'I'm all right Doctor,' she said. 'It's the baby.'

'Yes, I'm going to take a look now. Kate, give me the child, and ring Julie.'

Richard examined the baby carefully. It had all the signs and symptoms of peri-natal jaundice.

'When was the child born?' he asked quickly.

'About three hours ago, Doctor,' said the father. 'I delivered it.'

'But didn't you have any medical help?'

'Oh no, Doctor, we live out in the bush, about a hundred miles from here. You see, I'm an anthropologist, and I'm studying a primitive tribe. We try to live a natural life, so that they'll trust us. I delivered our first child a year ago and there were no problems at all.'

'I see,' said Richard thoughtfully. 'Have you and your wife had any blood tests?'

'No, you see we're perfectly healthy, Doctor. I delivered our first child and . . .'

'Yes, quite, now if you'll just sit down here we'll see what we can do. Nurse, bring me the blood-test tray.'

Ten minutes later Richard was on the phone to Kyruba hospital. 'Give me the night superintendent . . . Richard Brooks here . . . Oh it's you, Margaret. Listen, I've got a slight problem. We've got a rhesus baby, three hours old, needs a blood change. This place just doesn't have the equipment. Can I bring him down to you? Fine, OK. Be with you in half an hour.'

He put the phone down. 'Julie, you take charge here; Kate, you're coming with me.'

They drove down the road to Kyruba without speaking. Kate anxiously watched the tiny baby, as Richard skilfully dodged the potholes in the road. When they arrived at the hospital they were met by the night superintendent, a tall efficient-looking woman in her thirties.

'Hello, Richard,' she said. 'Everything's ready for you. This way please.'

'Sister Jones, this is Nurse Mathews,' said Richard, as Kate handed over the baby.

'Have you had any experience with rhesus babies?' asked Sister Jones.

'No, but I would like . . .' she started, when Richard broke in.

'I think it would be better if you and your staff assisted me, Sister. Nurse Mathews can wait in the staff common-room. It's down the corridor on the right. Now, Sister, let's get to work.'

They swept off down the corridor, leaving Kate feeling useless again. She went along to the common-room and sat down in a large armchair. She was furious with Richard. He seemed to enjoy humiliating her. Still it was nice to rest for a while . . . she closed her eyes and was soon fast asleep. Some time later she was awakened by the noise of the door closing. She sat up quickly and rubbed her eyes.

'Oh I'm sorry . . . I didn't mean to waken you,' said a deep soothing voice. It was Mike Gregson, his fair wavy hair tousled over his forehead. 'I got dragged out of bed for an emergency, but the nurses are coping now. What brings you here in the middle of the night?'

'I came down with Richard; he's doing a blood change on a rhesus baby.'

'All by himself?'

'Oh no, he's got Sister Jones and her staff. He didn't need me so I came in here for a rest.'

'Well, I'm glad you did. I was wondering when we were going to see you again. Knowing Richard, I thought he would probably keep you all to himself.'

'I really don't know what you're talking about. He never even notices me.'

'Oh come on; he loves having you around. I mean, why did he bring you instead of that other nurse . . . what's her name, Julie?'

'He brought me because Julie is midwifery-trained and I'm not. We've got a hypertensive pre-natal and a post-natal case. I couldn't possibly be left in charge.'

'Well, if you say so. I still think he fancies you.'

'Oh, don't be so silly. Besides, he's a happily married man,' Kate retorted.

Mike gave a loud guffaw. 'Is that what he told you?'

Kate was rather taken aback. 'Well, not in so many words, but he led me to believe . . .'

'Oh, he led you to believe, did he,' Mike interrupted her. 'Well listen here, my girl. If I were you . . .'

The door had opened quietly and Richard was standing there.

'You were saying, Mike?'

'Ah, hello, Richard.' Mike grinned mischievously at the irate figure in the doorway. 'I was just going to tell Kate how to take care of herself out here in the tropics.'

'I'm sure Kate is perfectly capable of taking care of herself.' Richard closed the door and sat down wearily.

'How did it go?' asked Kate.

'Very well. It's too soon to tell, but I think the baby will survive. We'll leave him here. The equipment is so much better.'

'You must get frustrated, stuck out there at Ikawa, Richard,' Mike said amiably.

'Yes I do. I shall be relieved when my six months is up.

Still it has it's compensations.' Richard smiled at Kate.

'I'm sure it has,' said Mike drily. 'I wonder if there's any coffee in this place. That's what I really came in for, before I was side-tracked by this charming young lady.'

He found a jar of instant coffee and a kettle. Outside the windows the sun was rising, casting a brilliant red glow into the room. Kate crossed the room and opened the windows on to the terrace. She could see the ships in the harbour, and the waves breaking on the harbour wall.

'It's so beautiful here in the early morning,' she said, when the two men joined her. 'I love Africa.'

'Then why don't you stay on?' said Mike. 'We're always short of nurses here.'

'Kate's got to go home to her fiancé,' said Richard.

'Lucky man,' said Mike.

They drank their coffee in silence, as they enjoyed the breathtaking view. People on the ships were beginning to wake up and move around, and Kate was fascinated to see everything come to life.

'I don't see how you can leave all this and go back to a dull life in the UK,' Mike said to her.

'Perhaps she's in love,' said Richard, and before Kate could reply he stood up. 'Let's see if we can find some breakfast; I'm starving.'

The three of them went to the staff dining-room and helped themselves to bacon and eggs.

'I never feel like breakfast unless I've been on duty during the night,' said Mike, sitting down next to Kate. As they were finishing their meal, Dr Miller walked in.

'My secretary told me you were here,' he said. 'It's good to see you again, Kate.'

Kate smiled. 'We enjoyed our day at Ogiwa. It was lovely to meet your delightful family.'

'That's why I came to find you. Helen is arranging a barbecue at the beach house on Sunday, and she especially wants you to come, Kate. How about you, Richard, are you free?'

'I wouldn't miss it for anything. But I'd better not leave Julie in charge on her own. Mike, would you stand in for me?'

'Anything to oblige a dear old friend,' said Mike cheerfully.

'Well, that's settled then,' said Dr Miller. 'I must dash. See you down at the harbour about ten.'

'Some people have all the luck,' said Mike, when Dr Miller had gone. 'Think of me cooped up at Ikawa when you're lying on the beach.'

'You'll have a marvellous day, with Julie hovering around you,' said Richard. 'You know she adores you.'

'Julie adores all men. I think she's getting desperate now. Thinks she's on the shelf. She must be all of twenty-five,' laughed Mike.

'Twenty-six, actually,' said Richard.

'Well, there you are, then. I'd better watch out. She might get her claws into me.'

'I think you're being perfectly horrid,' said Kate. 'You seem to think that all a girl thinks about is getting married.'

'Well you haven't wasted much time,' said Mike. 'I think you're much too young to settle down.'

'Exactly what I was telling her,' said Richard. 'She ought to look around and do something with her life, before she gets into a rut.'

'Oh, don't start that again,' said Kate. 'Come on, don't you think we should be getting back?'

'I think Richard should go back, and leave you here to do some real nursing,' said Mike. 'How about it Kate?'

'I've got a contract to finish at Ikawa,' said Kate firmly.

'And then you're going to be married. What a waste,' said Mike.

'OK, let's go,' said Richard. 'Enough of this idle chatter. What time can you make it to Ikawa on Sunday, Mike?'

'I'll try to get out about nine.'

'Fine, that'll give us time to get down to the harbour for ten o'clock.'

Richard and Kate went out to the Land Rover. The streets of Kyruba were busy, and the crowds spilled over from the narrow pavements. It was terribly hot, and they were forced to drive with the windows down even though the smell from the open drains was none too pleasant. Kate breathed a sigh of relief when they reached the edge of the town. The road became rougher as they drove towards Ikawa. Richard swerved to avoid a bush dog which streaked across in front of them.

'That was a near thing,' said Kate. 'Not the easiest road to drive on.'

'Do you drive?' asked Richard.

'No I'm afraid not. I'd like to learn, but not out here. David said he would teach me when I go home.'

'I wouldn't advise that.'

'Why not?'

'I tried to teach my wife, but it wasn't a success. In the end she went to a driving school. I don't think they were any good, but she passed her test eventually. Anyway I don't think women should drive.'

'Why ever not, for heaven's sake?' Kate gasped. 'Really, Richard, you do have the strangest ideas.'

'I don't think women are good drivers, that's all.'

'Rubbish. There's no earthly reason why women

shouldn't drive as well as men. I shall learn as soon as I get home.'

Richard pulled into the side of the road, and switched off the engine.

'I wish you wouldn't,' he said quietly.

'Do you mean you wish I wouldn't drive or you wish I wouldn't go home?'

'Both.'

Kate was surprised by the intensity of his voice.

'Richard, I must ask you something,' she said. 'Mike seemed amused when I said you were happily married. What was it you were going to tell me about your wife?'

'I don't want to talk about it just now.'

'But Richard, you were going to tell me when . . .' Kate started, but he interrupted her.

'I said I don't want to talk about it,' he snapped. 'I'm tired.'

He drove off at a furious pace. Neither of them spoke until they reached Ikawa.

'You'd better get some sleep, before you come on duty,' said Richard.

'Oh I'm perfectly OK,' Kate reassured him. 'I had a couple of hours in the staff room.'

'A couple of hours in an armchair is no good,' he said severely. 'I don't want you passing out on me. Go and have a good rest. I don't want to see you outside your room until at least four o'clock.'

With that he hurried away in the direction of the patients' wing.

Kate went to her room and closed the door thankfully. She felt lost and bewildered, and a little homesick. What a strange man Richard was, impossible to understand the way he treated her. She opened her drawer and took out the photo of David. Carefully she placed it on her dressing-table. Oh David, she thought, I wish I was at home with you. I always feel safe with you. Life isn't very exciting when we're together, but at least I know where I am.

She fell asleep as soon as her head touched the pillow. She dreamed she was in a maze and there was no way out. Every time she thought she had found an escape route she found it was a dead end. She woke up with a start to find Julie leaning over her.

'Whatever's the matter, Kate? I heard you calling out so I came in to investigate. Are you all right?'

Kate sat up. 'I was having such a weird dream. It's always difficult to sleep during the day. Thanks for coming in, Julie. What time is it?'

'Three o'clock. I was having a couple of hours off myself. Oh, what a super photo! Is that your fiancé?'

'Yes, that's David.'

'Wow, he's rather good-looking isn't he? How can you bear to be parted from him?'

'At this particular moment I'm missing him terribly.'

'I should think you are. Still, won't be long now. Some people have all the luck. You wouldn't see me sweating it out in the tropics if I was engaged to be married to such a gorgeous man,' Julie sighed. 'Everyone thinks I'm a career girl but I'd swop my starched apron for a little house in the country and a husband and kids, any day.'

'How's the rhesus negative mother?' asked Kate.

'Oh she's fine. Discharged herself this morning; Richard wanted to keep her in for a couple of days to check on her health, but she insisted on going with her husband. They went to Kyruba to see their baby, and then they were going to drive back to their home near the Kulani tribe. Quite mad. Imagine having a baby in such primitive conditions. Richard told them they're lucky their baby is alive.'

'And how's Mrs Benson?'

'She seems OK at the moment. Blood pressure a bit high this morning. I'm going on duty tonight, and Joseph will be there as well, just in case we have any more emergencies. Richard said could you cope with the evening session by yourself?'

'Of course I can. I'll go along now. Oh by the way, Julie, did Richard tell you John Miller has invited us to a beach picnic on Sunday?'

'He told me. I was going to have a moan about it, but then he said Mike Gregson was coming out to help, so I said I didn't mind at all.'

'You're sure?' Kate asked as she got out of bed and put on her uniform.

'Absolutely. Don't give it another thought. How are you getting on with Richard anyway?'

'He's terribly moody with me," said Kate cautiously.

'Oh really? I hadn't noticed. Perhaps he's missing his wife.'

'Perhaps,' said Kate quietly. 'I must go now.'

Kate went along to the patients' wing; Richard was sitting at the desk, writing a report on the rhesus baby. He looked up as she came in and smiled.

'My, am I glad to see you. It's been a long day.'

'Have you had any sleep?' Kate asked.

'Not yet, but I'm just going. Can you cope?'

'Of course I can. I'm not entirely useless you know. Besides I shall never get any experience if you don't give me some responsibility.'

'OK, I'm off then.' Richard got up and made for the door. 'Ring me if there's anything you can't handle.'

'Yes I will, of course.' Kate smiled, and went off to

start the evening round. It would have to be something really important before she would admit she needed his help.

CHAPTER FOUR

MIKE Gregson met them in the corridor on Sunday as they were finishing the morning round.

'Nice timing,' said Richard. 'We've just finished. Come and have a coffee.'

They went out on to the verandah. Musa appeared with the coffee pot and some cups and saucers.

'Before you go, is there anything you should tell me?' asked Mike, as he sipped the strong black brew.

'Julie knows what's going on. I don't think you'll be needed, unless Mrs Benson starts having problems again—she's our hypertensive mum-to-be,' said Richard. 'Otherwise I think you'll have a nice quiet day. You could probably have a swim in the pool this afternoon, if you can get Joseph to stand in for an hour or so. He's always happy to do some over-time.'

'I didn't know you had your own pool up here,' said Mike.

'Of course we have. You can't have a luxury nursing home without a pool,' laughed Richard. 'Some of our patients just come in for a rest-cure—Oh, that reminds me . . . pop in and see Mrs Marshall while you're here, Mike. She's in with nervous exhaustion again, and she enjoys chatting with young men. She gets terribly bored.'

'I thought I was here to minister to the sick, not to run a holiday camp,' said Mike, with a wry grin.

'Oh, you are, you are,' laughed Julie. 'Don't worry, I'll find you plenty to do.'

'OK, let's start now,' said Mike. 'Hadn't you two better be off, if you're going to meet John at ten?'

'We're just going—come on Kate.' Richard stood up impatiently. 'I'm going to collect my things. Meet me by the car in five minutes.'

Kate hurried to her room to change into a cool dress. She threw a bikini and a towel into her bag and dashed out to meet Richard. He was sitting in the car, with the engine running.

'At last,' he muttered, as Kate climbed in. He put the car into gear and they drove off. It was exactly ten o'clock when they arrived at the harbour. Richard parked the car and they went over to the waiting launch, where John Miller and his family were already on board. They were soon speeding over the blue water outside the harbour. The children jumped up and down excitedly as John steered the boat skilfully through the water, running along the coastline. After about half-an-hour they reached Tarkawa Bay. John ran the boat close to the shore and Richard jumped out to tie her up.

'It's so beautiful here,' said Kate as she helped Helen with the children. They removed their sandals and were paddling through the warm shallow water on to the beach.

'Oh I love it,' agreed Helen. 'We come here as often as John can spare the time.'

The men were loading the bags into large baskets and bringing them ashore.

'It's so peaceful,' continued Helen. 'We never see a soul. You can't get here except by water, so it's rather like a desert island.'

They went into a long low hut, built of dried grass and wooden poles. It felt pleasantly cool inside, after the heat of the sun.

'This belongs to the hospital staff,' explained Helen. 'Someone built it a few years ago, and we all help to keep it in good condition. I've brought all the food, of course, but everything else we need is here. How about a swim?'

They changed into bikinis and took the children into the sea. Kate stayed with Helen in the shallows, teaching the children to swim. They were soon joined by the men.

'Come on, Kate,' called Richard. 'I'll race you to the breakers.'

Kate looked out to where the high waves were breaking at the end of the shallow water. It looked dangerous, from where she was standing.

'I'm not a very good swimmer, Richard.'

'Nonsense; you don't need to swim once you get out there. It's as calm as a mill-pond beyond the waves. Come on, I'll show you. Just stay with me and you'll be OK.'

Kate obediently pushed herself forward in the turbulent water. The waves seemed to get stronger as they moved away from the shore. Richard swam slowly along by her side, making encouraging remarks.

'Fine, well done. Now just another few yards, and I promise you . . .'

'Oh Richard!' Kate suddenly screamed in terror as an enormous wave bore down as if to engulf them, 'I can't go through that one!'

'Yes you can. Head down, deep breath.' And then they were through the wave and out the other side. It was as Richard had predicted, as calm as a mill-pond. The waves were still pounding on the shore, but Kate and Richard lay on their backs, floating on the peaceful blue sea, which seemed to stretch for miles.

'Who would have thought it!' Kate laughed happily.

'Oh Richard, I was so scared on the way out here.'

'I know you were. I never thought we'd make it. But it was worth the effort, wasn't it?'

Kate smiled. There was no need to reply. It was absolute bliss to lie there with the sun shining down out of a cloudless sky and the buoyancy of the warm salt sea holding her up as if she were on a water mattress. A sudden movement on the surface of the sea caught her eye.

'Richard, look! What's that?'

A few yards away, two large fish jumped out of the water and dived back again in a graceful arc.

'Oh that's the porpoises. They're quite harmless. They seem to enjoy human company.'

'You're sure they're harmless?'

'Of course I'm sure. Let's go a bit nearer.'

They swam closer to the spot where the porpoises had risen out of the sea, only to see them swim further out.

'Don't let's go any further, Richard. I'm really not a very strong swimmer.'

'You don't need to worry. Just lie back and I'll carry you along. Relax now, you're as stiff as a board.' Richard took her firmly along through the water and soon she relaxed and closed her eyes. It was a marvellous feeling to be carried effortlessly through the water. Suddenly she realised they had stopped and she was leaning on Richard's chest. Quickly she pulled herself away and spun round in the water to face him.

'I thought you'd fallen asleep,' he said. 'You were so still.'

'Simply obeying orders to relax. I'm quite good at it, don't you think?'

'Mm. Shall we go a bit further out?'

Kate looked at the receding shore-line. 'No, I think that's far enough. I've never been so far from dry land before.'

'But you're quite safe with me here.' He smiled at Kate, and reached for her hand in the water.

'That's a matter of opinion,' laughed Kate.

'And what do you mean by that?' he said.

'Oh, never mind. Come on, let's go back now, before I lose my nerve.'

'OK, turn on your back. I'll take you as far as the breakers. After that you'll have to make it under your own steam, but I'll stay with you.'

Kate let Richard take her through the calm water. She was terribly aware of the nearness of his strong muscular body as he pulled her along. Once more she closed her eyes and abandoned herself to the sheer pleasure of the moment. All too soon she heard the sound of the breakers.

'All right Kate, now go along with this next wave and it should take you into shore. Ready? *Now!*'

Kate flung herself on to the crest of the wave and felt herself carried along by its momentous surge. She had no time to feel frightened, as she found herself speeding towards the shallow water. It was over in a few seconds and she laughed as she found herself on the shore with Richard at her side

'There, that wasn't too painful, was it?' he said.

'Oh, it was marvellous!'

John and the children came running towards them.

'My, that was a spectacular arrival,' said John. 'I thought you said you were a poor swimmer, Kate.'

'She's been taking swimming lessons,' said Richard.

'From a very good teacher,' Kate smiled at Richard. 'Thank you, I enjoyed it.'

'So did I,' he said.

'Well now,' Helen broke in, 'how about some lunch?'

'Rather. I'm starving,' said Richard. 'Can we help?'

'Yes; perhaps you and John would light the barbecue, and Kate and I will get the food organised.'

Kate and Helen went into the beach house and started to prepare the chicken and salad. Kate was suddenly aware that Helen was watching her.

'Kate, I'm glad you're getting on well with Richard. I haven't seen him so happy for a long time,' Helen said quietly. 'On the other hand, I'm a little worried about the fact that you're engaged. I wouldn't want to see him hurt.'

'Oh, it's a purely platonic friendship,' said Kate quickly. 'I mean it has to be. I'm engaged and he's married.'

'You mean he *was* married.'

'I thought he was still married.'

'He doesn't like to talk about it. His wife was killed in a car crash three years ago. He's never got over it, but today I felt there was something of the old Richard in him. He was happy again. And this is why I felt I had to warn you. I think he's falling in love with you.'

'No, I'm sure you're mistaken. We're just good friends—today that is. Sometimes he can be quite beastly to me. You wouldn't believe how horrid he can be.'

'Oh yes I would. And you see that's just his way of covering up his emotions. I think, because he likes you so much, he will often criticise you. Actually you remind me of his wife, Karen. I noticed it when we first met, and I was worried when you told me you were engaged. If he falls in love with you and then loses you too, I think it will be too much for him to cope with.'

'Helen, you really don't need to worry,' said Kate, reassuringly. 'Honestly, he is simply happy to be having a day out here with all of us. He knows I'm engaged. He's not going to get emotionally involved.' She paused for breath and looked at Helen. The two women smiled at each other.

'Come on, let's join the men,' said Kate, quickly, anxious to end the conversation. They carried the trays of food out to the place where Richard and John had lit the barbecue. Kate felt her heart pounding unbearably. She had tried to convince Helen; now she was trying to convince herself.

The barbecue was a great success. The chicken tasted delicious and they washed it down with a cold bottle of sparkling wine, which John produced from an improvised wine cooler. Afterwards they stretched out on rush mats in the shade of the palm trees. The children were playing in the sand but they soon became tired and started quarreling.

'I think I'd better put the children down for a rest in the beach hut,' said Helen, 'Otherwise they're going to be unbearable for the rest of the day.'

'Good idea,' said John, 'I'll come with you, I feel like a siesta myself.'

'I'm quite happy just lying here,' said Richard, lazily stretching himself and wiggling his toes in the sand. 'How about you, Kate?' He turned over to look at her.

'Mm?' Kate opened one eye. 'Yes; fine,' she murmured. 'I think I must have fallen asleep, it's the wine and the sun; it's making me so sleepy.'

'And all your swimming,' said Richard.

'Oh yes, let's not forget the swimming lesson,' laughed Kate. She was wide awake now, as she noticed Richard easing his body over towards her. Quickly she jumped to her feet.

'How about a run along the beach, to waken us up?' she said brightly.

Richard sat up, reluctantly. 'If that's what you want to do. Or another swim?'

'Much too soon after lunch,' said Kate. 'Later. Come on, let's run as far as the rocks.'

She set off at a good pace and it was several seconds before Richard caught up with her. They slackened the pace to a steady jog and ran side by side along the edge of the water. Soon they were clambering over the rocks which led round to another bay. The sand was glistening white in the afternoon sun. They sank down in the shade of the trees at the edge of the bay.

'This is the life,' said Richard. 'Can you imagine how chilly it would be if we were in England now? I think you're quite mad to think of leaving Africa.'

He had raised himself up and was leaning on one elbow, looking down on her. Kate grinned up at him.

'Ah, we're back to the usual conversation. I wondered when you would start that again. I can't think why you keep thinking about it. I'm here for six months, then I'm going back to England to be married, and that's all there is to it.'

'But I just don't feel that you're utterly committed to your engagement.'

Kate sat up quickly. 'Oh I see; you expect me to behave like a vestal virgin, because I'm engaged. I still have feelings you know. I can't help behaving like a woman. I do enjoy the company of other men. Is that so terrible?'

'No, I think it's marvellous. I just want to know where I stand, that's all.'

'Stand? You don't stand anywhere, Richard. I thought because you were married that sort of question wouldn't arise, but now that I know you're free, I suppose I'll have to think again. I was sorry to hear about your wife, Helen told me.'

'Did she,' he said quietly. 'I was going to tell you myself, but I hate talking about it. You know, you remind me of Karen.'

'That's what Helen said. But I'm not Karen, Richard. You'll have to start living in the present, and forget the past.'

'I know, and the present looks quite good to me—and the future, if only we could change one or two minor details.'

'One or two minor details?' asked Kate.

'Yes, the minor detail of your engagement to a man you don't love.'

'How do you know whether I love David, or not? I do love him, I do.' Kate found she was crying in her effort to convince Richard. She started to stand up, but he held her back, and taking her in his arms he pressed his lips gently against her sobbing mouth. For one brief moment she resisted and then, overcome by the warmth of his embrace, she responded. His strong arms were caressing her body. She felt a surge of desire, running through her. His hands were exploring her body. His head bent down, kissing her all over, and his tongue began licking the salt from her sunburnt skin, while his hand fondled her knee. Slowly his fingers brushed along the inside of her thigh . . . Suddenly she pulled herself away. 'Richard this is madness. You know we can't go on like this.'

He tried to pull her towards him again, but she stood up, shaking the sand from her body. Richard lay on the sand looking up at her. Slowly he drew himself up to his full height and placed his arms gently around her. She stiffened and made as if to break away, but his calm voice reassured her.

'Don't worry, Kate. It's up to you now, it's your decision. Go back to your fiancé. Have a marvellous life in some dreary old village. Have a couple of kids and be a good wife and mother. Oh, you'll love it.' His voice was hard and mocking now. The steely grey eyes pierced into her. He turned and walked off towards the sea.

'Richard, wait, can't we discuss it?'

He turned briefly. 'I don't think there's anything to discuss,' he said 'I'm going for a swim.'

'I'll come with you,' she called.

'If you like,' he said indifferently, and plunged into the water.

Kate followed and swam after him, but he was too quick for her. He swam far out beyond the breakers, and she did not attempt to reach him. The magic of the day seemed to have vanished. Sadly she went back to the shore.

There seemed no point in waiting around for Richard, so Kate walked slowly back to Tarkawa Bay. The Miller family were still having their siesta in the beach hut so she lay down in the shade of the plam trees and closed her eyes. The sound of the waves breaking on the shore reminded her of their morning swim. It seemed so long ago now. The heat of the afternoon sun made her drowsy and she fell asleep until the sound of the children playing nearby woke her up.

'Hello,' Helen called to her. 'Did you have a good walk?'

'Yes, it was very pleasant. I felt quite tired afterwards.'

'Where's Richard?' asked Helen.

'Oh, he went for a swim—too far for me, so I came back here.'

'I see,' Helen was looking at her quizzically. 'Everything all right?'

'Of course, why shouldn't it be?' said Kate brightly.

'I just wondered if you'd told Richard you knew about Karen.'

'Oh yes, I told him.'

'And . . . ?' Helen continued.

'And nothing,' Kate smiled. 'I told you there's no need to worry about Richard. He's perfectly capable of taking care of himself.'

John Miller came out of the beach hut and started to gather up the barbecue things. 'I think we'd better be packing up, dear,' he said to Helen. 'Where's Richard?'

'Apparently he went for a long swim.'

'All the afternoon?' John looked anxiously at his watch. 'Perhaps I'd better go and look for him.'

'I'll come with you,' said Kate, not wanting to be left alone with Helen to question her again.

They set off along the beach towards the rocks. As they started to climb over them Richard came into sight. He was sitting on a large rock at the water's edge, gazing out to sea.

'Richard,' called John, 'Are you all right?'

Richard turned towards them, as if in a trance, then he stood up and came over the rocks to meet them.

'We were getting a little worried about you,' said John.

'Sorry about that. I went for a long swim'. Richard had resumed his normal composure. He did not even look at Kate. The three of them walked back along the beach to where Helen was organising the baskets ready for the return journey.

They all helped to load the boat and then climbed aboard. John steered them out of the bay and turned towards Kyruba harbour. The sun was beginning to sink down into the sea, casting a dark red glow over the water.

'It's been such a lovely day,' said Helen. 'I always feel sad when we leave Tarkawa Bay.'

'So do I,' said John. 'Are you coming back for a sundowner, Richard?'

'Oh yes, you must,' put in Helen. 'You look as if you need something to revive you after your long swim.'

'Well, I was thinking I might . . .' Richard started to say, but John broke in with,

'Fine, fine. That's settled then. You can have a shower to get the salt off your skin, as soon as we get back—you too Kate.'

Kate was beginning to feel that the day had been long enough, but there seemed no way of escaping now. She climbed into the car beside Richard, when they reached Kyruba. They drove out to Ogiwa House without speaking.

This is ridiculous, thought Kate. We can't go on like this. Still, she decided, let him be the first to break the silence. Richard looked straight ahead at the road and said nothing.

When they arrived, Helen showed Kate into a small guest room, where she showered and changed. As the warm soapy water splashed over her body, she started to revive again. She put on her cool cotton dress and sandals and brushed out her long dark hair, before going down to meet the others on the verandah. An ice-cold gin and tonic was waiting for her and soon she began to feel that it had, after all, been a good day. Richard smiled across at her.

'Your sun-tan has improved today,' he said pleasantly. 'You're going to be a marvellous colour before you go home.'

'Yes it really suits you,' said Helen, admiringly, 'I never get a good tan. I'm too fair-skinned.'

'You're the typical English rose, my dear,' said John. 'Kate is the mysterious dusky maiden type.'

'I don't think I'm all that mysterious,' laughed Kate.

'Of course not,' said John. 'Still I do think this tropical climate suits you. How long did you say you are staying out here?'

'Six months.'

'Only six months. What a pity. Still, I suppose you could always bring your husband out for a holiday, after you're married. Helen and I would love to meet him. He must be quite a guy to have captivated someone like you.'

Kate raised her eyes and saw that Richard was watching her. Her gaze did not falter. Quietly she said,

'Yes he is. He's quite a guy, and I love him very much.'

Richard looked away so that she could not see the expression in his eyes. Helen went off to put the children to bed and the three of them sat quietly watching the sunset. Soon it was dark and Richard rose to go.

They took their leave of the Millers and set off on the road to Ikawa. Richard's hands gripped the steering wheel tightly and he did not look at Kate as he drove quickly back to Ikawa where Julie and Mike were waiting for them.

Richard insisted on going round the patients, even though they assured him there was nothing to do. Afterwards they all had supper in the cool dining-room, overlooking the inner garden.

'Did you have a good day?' asked Julie.

'Marvellous,' said Richard. 'I taught Kate how to ride the waves without a surf-board.'

'Sounds very complicated,' said Julie.

'No it's not really,' said Kate. 'You just hurl yourself on the top of the wave and it carries you into shore. All you need is confidence.'

'And Richard gave you confidence, I suppose,' said Mike.

'Yes he did,' she said quietly. 'How was your day?'

'Oh, very quiet. We worked all morning, and lazed around the pool this afternoon. I chatted to Mrs Marshall this evening and her nervous exhaustion seems to have disappeared completely,' said Mike.

'We ought to take you on to our permanent staff,' said Richard. 'You've got such a marvellous bedside manner.'

'Oh it's much too boring for me,' laughed Mike. 'Anyway, I hear you may not be here too long yourself. John Miller was telling me.'

'Yes, yes,' interrupted Richard. 'We'll talk about that some other time, Mike. It's been a long day. I'm going to turn in and have an early night. Goodnight everybody.' He went off across the darkened garden towards his room.

'He looks all in tonight,' said Mike. 'What ever have you been doing to him, Kate?'

'I think he's in one of his depressed moods,' said Kate. 'I was talking to Helen and she told me about his wife being killed in a car crash. You obviously knew about it, Mike.'

'Yes I did, but he doesn't like to talk about it. It would be better if he did. I think they were very much in love.'

'Do you suppose he'll ever marry again?' said Julie.

'Who knows,' said Mike. 'If the right girl came along, I'm sure he would.'

'I'm going to bed,' said Kate quietly. 'Goodnight Mike, goodnight Julie.' She went to her room and lay down on the bed. It seemed like a lifetime since she had left it. She remembered the ecstasy she had felt in Richard's arms. It must have been the wine and the sea and the sun, she thought. It couldn't be anything more . . .

CHAPTER FIVE

KATE needn't have worried about being alone with Richard. He seemed to be avoiding her. They met only when their professional duties coincided and then he was barely polite to her. Sometimes she found herself wishing she could catch a glimpse of the warm personality he had revealed during their day at Tarkawa Bay, but she told herself it was better this way. It would make it easier for her to return to David when her contract was finished.

Two months went by very quickly. Kate felt that she had learned very little about tropical nursing, but some of the general nursing would be useful to her when she returned to England. Mrs Benson had a healthy baby boy and Kate helped with the delivery. She decided that somehow she must try to fit in her midwifery training before she married David.

Musa brought in the morning post one day as they were all sitting round the breakfast table. It was always exciting to receive letters from England and Kate was pleased to find there were two addressed to her. She recognised David's handwriting on one, but the other was unknown to her. She opened it and found, to her surprise, it was from Dr Clark.

'How nice,' she said to Julie. 'I didn't expect Dr Clark to write to me. I suppose he's going to tell me about his visit to Mummy.' She started to read it to herself.

'Dear Kate, I hope you are enjoying your time at Ikawa. I am having a marvellous holiday. I have done absolutely nothing except enjoy myself, especially since calling to see your mother. She has asked me to write to you. As you know, your mother and I were friends during your father's lifetime, when we all lived in Matala. I always admired her, and when we met soon after your father's death, I found that my admiration had turned to love. I asked her to marry me, but she said it was too soon and she felt that she could never love anyone but your father. Now, after all these years we have met again, and we are both very much in love. We are going to be married next month, and then I shall retire and take your mother to live with me in Scotland.

'I hope all this will not be too much of a shock for you. We see no point in waiting any longer—we are neither of us getting any younger!

'We are hoping that you will come home for the wedding. I have taken on another trained nurse, so that you will be free to travel home as soon as you like. She will arrive at Ikawa on 20th June. Could you arrange for Buba to be at the airport to meet the 4 o'clock plane.

'Your mother sends her love, and we are both looking forward to seeing you soon. Yours affectionately, James Clark'

'Phew . . .' Kate sank back in her chair.

'What's the matter? asked Julie.

'You'll never believe it. Dr Clark is going to marry my mother. The wedding's next month.'

'No kidding! Why that's marvellous. How do you feel about it?' said Julie.

'I don't know. It hasn't really sunk in yet.'

Richard put down the letter he was reading. 'It's amazing how excited you girls get about a wedding.'

'Yes, but this is really something special,' said Julie. 'It will be so nice for your mother not to be alone.'

'Will you go home for the wedding?' he asked.

'Of course I will. Dr Clark is sending another nurse to replace me. She's arriving on 20th June—Oh heavens! that's today.'

'Not another novice to train,' groaned Richard. 'I've only just got you organised, Kate. I suppose you'll stay on in England after the wedding.'

'Oh no—I shall come back to finish my contract.'

'I'm sure Dr Clark would release you from it, if you asked him,' he said evenly.

'I would prefer to come back,' said Kate quietly.

'Ah, but what if your beloved fiancé insists you stay?' the mocking tone was back in his voice.

'I don't think he will,' Kate said coolly as she stood up and started to walk over to the reception area. 'I must go and find Buba, to arrange for him to meet the plane.'

'Well I hope he makes a better job of it than he did when I came out,' said Richard.

Kate did not reply.

The morning routine occupied all her attention and she had no time to think about the wedding until after lunch. It was very quiet as everyone was taking the usual siesta, but Kate found she could not rest in her room. She wandered out across the garden and made for the swimming pool. It was deserted. She went into one of the changing rooms and put on her bikini.

The cool water relaxed her as she plunged in and swam a couple of lengths. Shaking the water from her body, she stretched out on one of the chairs in the shade of the trees and closed her eyes. All around the pool she could hear the insects droning in the garden. It was calm and peaceful and she was almost asleep, when she heard someone diving into the water.

It was Richard. He swam several lengths before he noticed her. From the middle of the pool he called out, 'Come along in; it's beautifully cool.'

'No, I've had my swim,' she said.

'Don't be lazy. Come in and I'll give you another swimming lesson.'

'No thanks, I was just going, actually.'

'Don't go just yet.' Richard climbed out of the pool and came over to her chair. He sank down on to the one next to her.

'I expect you're longing to be home again,' he said pleasantly.

'Yes, it will be nice to see everyone again.'

'Everyone?'

'Well there's my mother, grandmother and all the relatives . . . and David.'

'Especially David. He's a very lucky man.'

'Do you think so?' She looked him straight in the eye.

'Yes, I do,' he replied quietly.

Kate started to move off her chair. This was beginning to be a difficult situation again. She had promised herself to avoid being alone with Richard and now here she was once more lying next to him. He put his hand on her arm as she started to rise.

'I get the impression you've been avoiding me, since our last swim at Tarkawa,' he said.

'You could say that,' she said quietly.

'There's no need to worry. I'm not going to force myself on you again. I think I underestimated your love for your fiancé. I must admit I thought you had just got yourself engaged to the first man who came along, but it's obviously more than that. I'm sorry if I upset you at Tarkawa. It won't happen again.'

He got up from his chair and strolled over into the

garden. Kate remained quite still. She should be feeling relieved, but instead she felt sad. As she watched the tall handsome figure walking away, the tears sprang into her eyes.

Desperately she jumped up and plunged into the pool. Richard turned as he heard the splash.

'I thought you didn't want to swim anymore,' he called as she surfaced.

'Changed my mind,' she called back.

'Woman's prerogative, I suppose,' he said, and walked off across the garden.

As soon as he was out of sight she climbed out and went back to her room. It was almost time for the arrival of the new nurse, so she put on her uniform and went along to reception.

The screech of brakes in the drive told Kate that Buba had returned from the airport. She went to the main door and out on to the steps. A tall, slim blonde was getting out of the car. Buba had already started to unload the numerous pieces of luggage from the boot. He called out to Kate,

'This be the new nurse, madam.' There was no disguising the admiration he felt for this elegant and beautiful young woman. Kate went down the steps to greet her.

'Hello, I'm Kate Mathews. Welcome to Ikawa.'

'Liz Mason,' she said, stretching out a well-manicured hand. 'Quaint little place, isn't it? I didn't know what to expect so I've brought the lot.' She indicated the suitcases which were being taken up the steps by Buba and Musa.

'However did you get them all on the plane?' said Kate.

'Daddy paid excess baggage for them. I mean, one has

to keep up standards hasn't one, even out here in the jungle.'

'I'll show you to your room,' said Kate.

'Yes, please do that. I'm absolutely exhausted. I need a long hot bath.'

'I'm afraid you've only got a shower in your room, but there are baths in the patients' wing.'

'How very primitive. Oh well, I suppose I'll just have to get used to roughing it.' She sighed deeply as she followed Kate inside. As they were walking down the corridor, Richard came out of his room. Kate made the introductions, and noticed that Richard held on to Liz's hand just a little longer than necessary.

'We are delighted to welcome you, Nurse Mason,' he said.

'Oh please, call me Liz.' She flashed him a warm smile.

He smiled back at her. 'Did you have a good journey?'

'Monstrous—I hate travelling by air. I need a long relaxing bath, but Kate tells me you've only got showers.'

'There's a bathroom next to my room, if you'd like to use it. I'll show you the way.'

'Oh that's marvellous.'

They went off down the corridor, and Kate felt that she was not needed any further. She went on to the patients' wing and started the evening round. When she called in to see Chief Ladipo she found him walking round the room on his crutches. He beamed a welcoming smile when she went in.

'See how clever I am,' he said 'Dr Brooks says I can go home tomorrow.'

'That's good news. We shall miss you though.'

'You must come out to see me—only ten miles away.

Bring Dr Brooks, or he can bring you,' he laughed. 'He's a very nice man, don't you think so?'

Kate smiled. 'Yes, I think so.'

'I think you like him a lot, don't you.'

'Oh really,' she laughed. 'What is this—some kind of third degree? I think it's high time you were going home.' Kate started to remake his bed, plumping the pillows energetically.

'But you will come and see me, won't you Nurse?'

'I'll try; now let's get you back into bed.'

She continued on round the patients until it was time to go off duty. When she had changed out of her uniform she joined the others on the verandah for a drink. Liz was sitting next to Richard, talking about the pleasures of cruising.

'I can't bear aeroplanes,' she was saying 'They give me claustrophobia, I like to spread out in my own cabin with a sea view. What do you think, Kate?'

'Actually, I've never travelled by sea.'

'Really? How amazing . . . Daddy and I take a cruise every winter, I love the sea. That was really why I came out here. I thought a few months in the sun would do wonders for my tan.'

'You might have to do a little work,' said Julie dryly.

'Don't frighten her,' said Richard. He turned to Liz. 'I think you'll find it very pleasant out here. The work is easy compared with hospital routine in the UK.'

Liz stretched her long slim legs and smiled at Richard. 'I'm sure I shall enjoy myself. What's the night life like?'

'Night life?' Julie and Kate looked at each other and burst out laughing.

'Yes, night life,' repeated Liz.

'Well you can watch the lizards in the garden, or try to catch a land crab or . . .'

'It's not as bad as that, Kate' interrupted Richard. 'If you enjoy night life, Liz, there's plenty in Kyruba. I'll take you down there one evening. You mustn't go alone.'

'Of course not. Thank you, Richard, I should enjoy that.'

'How about tomorrow? I've got to visit Kyruba hospital in the afternoon and we can stay on and see the sights afterwards.'

'Fine, I'll look forward to it.'

Liz and Richard continued to talk to each other as if they were old friends. It was a relief for Kate and Julie when Musa came to tell them supper was ready.

After supper Kate went to her room to write to Dr Clark. The sound of laughter drifted across the garden. I'll go home next week she thought, then I can help Mummy get ready for the wedding.

Next day Liz was introduced to the patients and the normal nursing routine continued, except that they had another pair of hands. Liz, however, was very careful what she did with her hands. She wore surgical gloves most of the time, so as not to spoil her manicure, and moaned loudly if she had to do anything with her bare hands.

'It's bad enough having to keep my nails short, without getting the skin roughed up.'

'What made you become a nurse?' said Kate as the two of them were having lunch.

'Curiosity, I suppose, and I used to think the uniform looked so glamorous. Well I had to do something between school and getting married. Otherwise I should get so bored.'

'You're getting married, are you?' asked Kate.

'Isn't everyone? I mean I've got nothing planned. I'm

just waiting for the right man to come along. I've got plenty of time—I'm only twenty-three. How about you?'

'I'm engaged actually.'

'Good heavens, what on earth are you doing out here?'

'I wanted to do some travelling before I settled down. I used to live here when I was a child.'

'When's the wedding?' Liz asked.

'We haven't fixed a date yet.'

'You don't seem very thrilled about it. When I get myself engaged it will have to be someone absolutely fantastic—older than me of course; experienced, handsome and terribly rich.'

Julie and Richard arrived at that moment and sat down.

'Who are you talking about?' asked Julie.

'The man I shall marry,' said Liz.

'Happy hunting,' said Julie.

'I'm not doing the hunting. I shall wait to be hunted.' She turned to Richard and smiled. 'What time do we leave this afternoon?'

'As soon as we've had lunch. We shall be at the hospital if you need me girls.'

'Fine,' said Kate. 'I think Julie and I can cope. Oh Richard, I've decided to go home next week, if that's all right with you.'

'Yes of course, Liz will be able to step into your shoes, won't you Liz?' He turned towards Liz and smiled at her. She returned his smile and said, 'Delighted, Richard.'

Kate and Julie shared the work between them for the rest of the day. There were no emergencies, so they left Joseph on night duty and had an early night. Kate felt exhausted as she lay down on her bed. She was about to switch off the light by her bedside when the phone rang. It was Mike Gregson.

'Kate, is Richard taking you to the hospital ball?'

'I didn't know there was one.'

'So you've not been invited yet?'

'Most certainly not. When is it?'

'Next Wednesday. Will you come with me?'

'Well I'd like to, Mike, but it's the night before I go home.'

'Go home? That's a bit sudden, I thought you were here until October.'

'Oh this is just a flying visit. My mother's getting married to Dr Clark.'

'Really? How amazing! Well, that's a good excuse to celebrate, so you must definitely come with me. I won't take no for an answer.'

'Mike, you're very sweet, but . . .'

'Kate, we'll have a marvellous time. It will do you good. I'll pick you up about eight. 'Bye for now.'

Kate lay back on her pillow. She found herself looking forward to the ball; Mike was such fun to be with, and so much less complicated than Richard.

Across the garden she heard the screech of brakes on the gravel drive, and the slamming of car doors. Liz and Richard had returned from their night on the town. From the sound of their laughter they were enjoying themselves immensely.

CHAPTER SIX

NEXT morning at breakfast Liz and Richard told Kate and Julie about their hilarious evening visiting the night spots of Kyruba.

'Honestly, Kate, I've never been in such weird places,' said Liz. 'We went to this dreadful little wine bar—would you believe, it was called Chez Simon? Imagine, Chez Simon, out here in the jungle!' and the peals of laughter rang out again. 'Richard ordered some champagne—champagne! When it arrived it tasted like diluted lemonade—and it was warm!'

'Of course, I sent it back,' put in Richard, 'and we finished up drinking gin and tonic. Not much they could do to spoil that.'

'Then there was this awful sailor, came up and asked me to dance—he was blind drunk, Richard told him to go away, and I thought there was going to be a fight. What a night!'

'But you enjoyed yourselves, nevertheless,' said Julie.

'Oh absolutely! Wouldn't have missed it for anything. I could do without the hangover though,' said Liz.

'Why don't you take the morning off?' said Richard solicitously. 'I'm sure the girls can manage without you, can't you, girls?'

'No problem,' said Kate quickly. She found Liz's help something of a mixed blessing.

'That's terribly sweet of you. Well, I'll toddle off back to bed and catch up on my beauty sleep. Thanks awfully.' And Liz drifted back to her room.

The three of them quietly finished breakfast. As they were walking along to the patients' wing, Richard said, 'Oh, by the way, have you girls heard about the hospital ball next week?'

'Yes, Mike phoned me last night to see if I would go with him. Of course I said I'd be delighted, even though it is the night before I go back to England.'

'I thought I would take Liz,' said Richard hurriedly. 'It will be nice for her to get to know the hospital staff. What about you, Julie?'

'What about me?' said Julie.

'Well, have you been invited?'

'No.'

'Would you mind holding the fort for us?'

'Not at all. I don't mind playing Cinderella while you all go to the Ball.' Julie tried to make it sound like a joke, but there was a bitterness in her tone.

'Yes, I'm sorry about it, but we'll try to make it up to you.'

'Oh sure,' Julie said as they went into the first patient's room. 'Don't worry about me. I can take care of myself. I've had plenty of practice.'

Kate could not help feeling sorry for Julie. During the next few days she watched her anxiously and tried to be as kind and helpful as she could.

On the evening of the Ball, Julie turned to her and said, 'I'm going to miss you, Kate. It's going to be hell, stuck out here with those two love-birds.'

'I know,' said Kate sympathetically, 'But I won't stay home long—a couple of weeks at the most.'

'Fine. Honestly, sometimes I can't think why I'm still out here. I think I might go home when my contract finishes at the end of the year. Anyway, I hope you have a good time tonight. What time is Mike picking you up?'

'About eight. I'd better go and get ready.'

'Yes, don't keep Prince Charming waiting.'

Kate went to her room and showered and changed. She had already packed her suitcases for the morning, and they stood by the door, reminding her that tomorrow she would be with David and her family. She put on her evening dress which was in white taffeta, off-the-shoulder, and looked very attractive with her deep tan.

Mike whistled as she came out on to the verandah. 'Wow, you look stunning.' He was having a drink with Richard and both men stood up as she joined them.

'Where's Liz?' asked Kate, as she accepted a drink from Musa.

'She said she'd be along in a minute' said Richard. 'That was about an hour ago.'

'Women!' said Mike 'Can't think why they take so long. Oh, here she comes.'

Liz was wearing a tight-fitting black dress with a deep slit up the side, and very high strappy black sandals. Richard rushed to hold a chair for her.

'You look absolutely stunning, Liz. I couldn't think why you were taking so long,' he said as he handed her a drink. 'But now I see it was all worth it.'

'I had the most terrible time—I broke a nail,' she moaned.

Kate looked at Mike, and the two of them burst out laughing.

'What's so funny?' said Liz.

'Oh nothing,' said Kate. 'I was just thinking what a traumatic experience you must have had.'

'I had to go along to the patients' wing to ask Julie for something to stick on it. Then I had to redo all my nails in a different colour. It took ages.'

'I'm sure it did,' said Mike. 'Never mind, you're here

now and we're all going to have a marvellous evening. Whose car shall we take, Richard?'

'We'd both better take our own. There's no point you coming back here afterwards, to pick up your car.'

'But I'd like to come back; maybe have a nightcap with you.'

'Suit yourself. I still think we need our own cars. I can bring both the girls back, and you can stay on at Kyruba.'

'Lucky old you, with these two gorgeous girls. Come on, let's go. We'll take my car, Kate, and I can decide whether to drive you back later.'

Mike's car was a two-seater sports model, with the roof down. They drove off at a high speed, scattering the gravel on the drive as they went.

'Quite a girl, that Liz,' said Mike. 'Richard seems to have fallen for her hook, line and sinker.'

'Yes, they spend all their off-duty time together,' said Kate quietly.

'Quite surprising, really,' said Mike. 'I mean she's not really his type—much too flashy. If you ask me he's just putting on an act.'

'Putting on an act?' queried Kate. 'What do you mean?'

'I should have thought it was obvious.'

'No, it's not obvious. Mike, what are you talking about?'

'Oh, forget it,' said Mike, 'Let's not spoil the evening.'

They drove to the hospital in silence, and parked the car in the car park near the main hall. The sound of music and laughter drifted across through the palm trees, along the edge of the gardens. They walked quickly up to the main entrance and went inside. Mike found a table near the dance floor and then whisked Kate on to the floor. As they danced round the floor,

Kate saw Richard and Liz coming through the door. Liz caused quite a stir in her stunning dress and Richard seemed proud to be escorting her.

He introduced her to John Miller and his wife and they sat down at their table. Mike and Kate returned to their own table.

'Did you see Richard and Liz making their entrance?' said Mike.

'Couldn't miss it,' said Kate dryly.

'Let's go and join them,' said Mike.

'Do you think that's a good idea?' said Kate quickly.

'Of course it is,' said Mike. 'Besides, I want to ask Liz for a dance.' They walked across the floor to John Miller's table. He stood up when he saw Kate and kissed her lightly on the cheek.

'My dear, you're looking marvellous, isn't she, Helen?'

'As always,' smiled his wife. 'I'm so glad you could come, I thought Richard must have left you back at Ikawa.'

'No, poor old Julie is playing Cinderella tonight,' said Kate.

'Won't do her any harm,' Mike said. 'Besides, we couldn't leave the gorgeous Liz at home.'

Liz smiled at Mike and he took her hand. 'May I have this dance with you?'

'Of course,' She stood up, aware of the admiring glances around her as she walked on to the floor.

As Liz and Mike glided off, John Miller turned to his wife and said, 'Shall we dance this one, my dear?' Helen stood up and followed her husband, leaving Richard and Kate alone at the table.

'I don't want to dance this one, do you?' said Richard.

'Well, not if you put it like that.'

'I'm sorry, I didn't mean to be rude. I just thought it would be nice to sit and talk together for a while. After all, I may not see you again after tomorrow.'

'But I'm coming back.'

'Are you? You don't have to,' he said firmly.

'I ought to finish my contract, and I've promised Julie I'll return. She's not too happy at the moment.'

'Really? I hadn't noticed.'

'No, I don't suppose you have,' said Kate quietly. 'I hope Liz will pull her weight while I'm away.'

'I'm sure she will,' said Richard. 'She's a·charming girl, don't you think?'

'Absolutely,' Kate forced herself to smile. This small talk was becoming very trying. He seemed like a stranger to her, Mike was right; Richard was putting on an act. She could hardly remember what the real man was like.

'Can I get you a drink?' he asked politely.

'I'll come with you,' said Kate. Anything was better than sitting at the table making conversation. They crossed over to the bar. Richard seemed to know everyone, and everyone wanted to have a few words with him. The main question they asked was when was he coming back to Kyruba hospital.

'You can't stay out in that backwater too long,' said Margaret Jones, the night-sister whom Kate had met during the rhesus baby emergency. 'You'll get rusty, Richard.'

'Don't worry, I've got plans,' smiled Richard. 'I've no intention of staying there much longer.'

'I heard a little rumour . . .' she started to say, but Richard stopped her.

'Yes, OK, thank you Margaret. Just keep your little rumour to yourself.' He smiled amiably at the listening crowd around the bar. 'Let's have another drink. My shout, I think.'

At that moment Mike and Liz came across to join them. Richard introduced Liz to his friends who were all impressed by his apparent conquest. Mike asked Kate to dance and she was relieved to leave Richard and Liz to their mutual admiration. The evening seemed to pass quickly after that, Kate danced with John Miller and several of Mike's friends.

When it came to the last waltz, she was surprised to find Richard standing in front of her. He smiled his most charming smile and reached for her hand. 'Will you dance with me, Kate?'

Her legs suddenly felt like jelly. This was the Richard she had glimpsed briefly, before they had decided to go their separate ways. He took her in his arms and they glided on to the floor. Kate closed her eyes for a few seconds and abandoned herself to the romantic feeling sweeping over her. She was brought down to earth quickly as Richard said,

'You must be looking forward to seeing David tomorrow.'

'Yes, yes I am,' she said brightly.

'Tomorrow night you'll be in his arms again. You'll have forgotten all about Ikawa and its problems.'

He held her briefly away from him so that he could watch her reaction. She returned his gaze with a brief smile, but did not reply.

They danced in silence until the music ended. It seemed to Kate that Richard was holding her just a little tighter than was necessary, but she did not try to loosen his clasp.

Liz was rather put out when they returned to the table. Apparently one of the young house surgeons had insisted on dancing with her and she had not enjoyed the experience.

'Richard, you might have told me you were going to leave me alone,' she said petulantly.

'Leave you alone!' he started irritably, and then the charming manner returned. 'Ah, my poor darling. I had to have the last dance with Kate; I may never see her again,' he smiled at Kate.

'Richard, I keep telling you, I shall be back in a couple of weeks,' she said.

'Oh really,' said Liz. 'I thought I was here to replace you.'

'Perhaps you can sort things out with Dr Clark when you see him, Kate,' said Richard, 'Now, where's Mike got to? Haven't seen him for ages.'

At that moment Mike hurried across the floor. 'Sorry to neglect you folks. I got buzzed to go on the wards. Slight emergency; anyway it's under control now but I'd better stay here at Kyruba. Can you handle the two girls on your own, Richard?'

'I shall be delighted.' Richard put an arm around the waists of Liz and Kate and escorted them to his car. Mike kissed Kate briefly on the cheek, 'Take care of yourself in England, and come back soon,' he said.

Richard put the car in gear and they drove off up the Ikawa road. Liz had made sure that she sat in the front, next to Richard, so Kate had to sit in the back. It was a beautiful evening and she found herself remembering the first time she had driven up this road with Richard. It seemed such a long time ago.

When they arrived back at Ikawa, Richard said he wanted to see if all was well with the patients. Liz thought this was rather tiresome.

'Honestly, Richard. Julie will call you if there are any

problems. I thought we were going to have a nightcap.'

'You go ahead and start without me. I shan't be long,' he said.

'There's no point sitting out here by myself,' said Liz crossly. 'I may as well go to bed.' With that she flounced across the garden towards her room. Richard watched her go; his face devoid of all expression. Then he turned to Kate. 'Shall we see if Julie's got some coffee on?' he said quietly.

'Only if you need me in a professional capacity,' she said.

'But of course. What else?' he smiled.

Together they made their way over to the patients' wing. Julie was sitting at the desk, reading. She jumped in surprise as they appeared, but she seemed pleased to see them. 'Hello, I didn't expect to see you tonight. Did you have a good time?'

'Marvellous,' said Richard. 'We came to see if all was well.'

'Fine, no problems. All the patients are asleep. I've had nothing to do for the past two hours.'

'Good, then perhaps you can make us some coffee.'

'I like that,' said Julie amiably. 'I do all the work and you come back demanding coffee.'

'I'll make it,' said Kate firmly.

'Oh yes. Kate makes very good coffee,' said Richard as they all went into the kitchen.

'Have you finished your packing?' asked Julie.

'Almost; I can't believe I shall be in England tomorrow.'

They drank their coffee and then Kate said she must get some sleep. 'It'll be a long day tomorrow.'

'Is David going to meet you at Heathrow?' asked Richard.

'Yes; he'll drive me back to Yorkshire.'

'You're so lucky,' said Julie. 'Think of me stuck out here doing all the work.'

'You'll have Liz to help you,' put in Richard.

'Oh yes, she'll be a great help, when she's not manicuring her nails.'

'Oh come now. Isn't that a little unfair?' said Richard.

'No, I don't think so,' said Julie firmly. 'I can't see her learning the ropes as quickly as Kate did.'

'Oh dear. Looks like I'm going to have staff problems, when you go, Kate,' moaned Richard. 'Perhaps you'd better come back.'

'I intend to,' said Kate quietly. 'I must go off to bed now. Goodnight.'

'I'll walk you across to your room,' said Richard. 'You might disturb a snake in the garden, at this time of night.'

'Never have done before,' laughed Kate. 'I always make a loud noise with my feet when I walk so that they know I'm coming.'

They walked together across the garden. The insects were droning all around them. It was still warm and the pleasant odour of frangipani floated in the air. Kate paused on the steps to her room and held out her hand to Richard. He took it and drew her close to him. She felt herself go limp with anticipation. He held her closely in his arms; she felt his body hard against hers. His hands began to caress her firmly but gently. She trembled with ecstasy and anticipation at what might follow.

'Kate, oh Kate,' he whispered. His parted lips sought and found hers; his tongue eased its way between her teeth and began the exploration of her eager mouth, heightening the passion as they remained locked together in an all-consuming embrace. Kate moved out of his arms and opened the door to her room. He started to follow her into the room, then, pausing on the step, he merely brushed his lips lightly on her cheek and turned quickly away. 'Goodbye,' he whispered. She watched him walk back across the garden to his own room.

'Goodbye,' she echoed softly.

CHAPTER SEVEN

RICHARD and Julie came out on to the steps to say goodbye to Kate next morning. Buba put her cases into the boot and started up the engine. As the car sped along to the airport, Kate sank back into the seat, feeling a mixture of sadness and excitement.

Several hours later, after an uneventful flight, she reached Heathrow. David was waiting for her and she rushed into his arms.

'Darling, it's so good to be back,' she breathed.

'Well, I'm glad about that,' said David. 'I thought you might want to stay out there forever. You're such a restless creature.' He held her to him for a moment then took a long look at her. 'Mm, you've lost weight. Much too skinny.'

'It's the heat. And we do work quite hard.'

'And play hard, I imagine. What was this you told me about a hospital ball last night? I would have thought an early night would have made more sense, considering you had a long journey in front of you.' David opened the car door for her and she climbed in.

'Don't be cross, David. You know I like dancing.'

'That's not the point. You look absolutely whacked. You ought to take more care of yourself. Close your eyes and have a little sleep.'

'Yes, Doctor,' Kate said and closed her eyes briefly. She had forgotten how David liked to fuss about her health. She opened her eyes and watched him as he steered the car through the traffic. His dark hair was neatly combed back, giving him a strong, reliable appearance. He looked like a successful family doctor already. Kate relaxed completely: it was good to feel cared for. Soon she fell asleep as David drove smoothly northwards. When she awoke, the countryside had changed to the soft limestone walls and green fields of the Yorkshire Dales.

'Goodness, that was a long sleep,' she said. 'I didn't know I was so tired.'

'You must have been exhausted,' said David. 'We're nearly there.'

Kate sat up and combed her hair.

The car was climbing up a steep hill and she waited breathlessly for the view of the valley at the other side. As they went over the brow of the hill she saw the fields spread out below them like a patchwork quilt. Her mother's farm looked like a matchbox toy. The car went slowly down the hill: David had changed into bottom gear so as not to overwork the brakes and Kate had time to soak in the charm of the valley. The setting sun was casting warm glowing rays over the fields. She could not imagine why she had ever wanted to leave home.

David put his hand on hers, 'It's good to have you back,' he said.

'It's good to be back,' she echoed.

Her mother rushed out of the house as the car drove up to the front door of the farmhouse.

'Darling,' she called delightedly. 'How lovely to see you again.' Mother and daughter hugged each other lovingly, and Kate found the tears were streaming down her cheeks.

'It's so good to be home,' she said.

'You look marvellous,' said her mother, 'What a fabulous suntan!'

'Yes, but she's much too thin,' put in David.

'Nonsense. It's fashionable to be thin,' said Kate's mother. 'She looks just right. Stop fussing, David. Come inside. We've waited dinner for you.'

Everyone was waiting for her in the sitting room, with its comfortable chairs, oak beams and chintz curtains. Dr Clark sprang to his feet as she entered.

'Lovely to see you again, Kate. You're looking as beautiful as ever,' he said as he embraced her warmly.

Her grandparents sat quietly on either side of the fireplace smiling serenely at their lovely grand-daughter. Kate had forgotten how frail they were. She went over and kissed them.

'Have you finished your travelling now, Kate?' said her grandmother anxiously.

'Well, not quite. I've got to go back until October, to finish my contract.'

'That's really not necessary,' said Dr Clark. 'I thought Nurse Mason had taken over from you.'

'I don't feel I've had long enough to learn much out there,' said Kate quickly. 'I really would prefer to return until October.'

'As you wish, my dear,' said Dr Clark. 'I'm pleased you're enjoying life in Matala.'

'If you ask me she's enjoying life too much out there,' said David. 'Hospital balls, beach barbecues—it sounds more like a holiday.'

'James, stop talking shop and open the champagne,' put in June Mathews amiably.

'Champagne?' said Kate. 'What's the celebration?'

'Your return to the fold of course, and my wedding,' said June happily.

The champagne cork flew out of the bottle and landed in grandmother's lap. Startled she held it out to Kate.

'Take this, my dear, and keep it for good luck. I expect we shall soon be celebrating your wedding.' She grinned mischievously towards David, who smiled and said,

'Yes, it won't be long now. As soon as Kate has stopped gallivanting round the world we'll name the day.'

'Good idea,' said Dr Clark. 'You're a lucky man, David.' He turned to Kate, 'Now tell me about Ikawa; how are things going?'

'Very well. Richard seems to have everything under control.'

'I knew he would have. He's a splendid doctor. There's no need to worry when he's around. And the new nurse?'

'Er . . . she seems to be coping all right.'

'You don't sound too sure. I had a few doubts myself, but I had to make a quick decision and the agency said she had good references from all the right people. Her father is a millionaire.'

'That doesn't necessarily make her a good nurse,' said David practically.

'Quite,' said Dr Clark. 'I hope I haven't made an unwise choice.'

'Richard seems to like her,' said Kate.

'Thank goodness for that,' said Dr Clark.

'I think Mrs Barnes is ready to serve dinner,' said June, looking towards the doorway, where the old housekeeper was hovering shyly.

'Yes, dinner's ready,' said Mrs Barnes. 'Welcome home, Kate.'

They all went into the dining-room with its long oak table and Welsh dresser displaying the willow-pattern carving dishes and dinner service. From the windows there was a magnificent view across the valley. It was almost dark, but the light of the moon glinted on the river. Kate felt happy to be back in the family home. David sat down next to her and squeezed her hand. 'I love you,' he whispered. Kate smiled back at him.

Dr Clark sat opposite them, and asked Kate endless questions about Matala. 'Tell me about the Hospital Ball, Kate,' he said 'Did you see John Miller.'

'Yes, he was there.'

'And how was he?'

'He seemed very well.'

'Good. I'm hoping he'll take over Ikawa from me, now that I've decided to retire.'

'You're leaving Ikawa?' asked Kate.

'Of course. You don't think I'm going to leave my beautiful bride and go back to the tropics, do you?' he laughed.

'I suppose not. I honestly hadn't thought about it. So what do you intend to do?' said Kate.

'Do? Why absolutely nothing, except enjoy myself. I shall run my estate in Scotland, do some fishing, a little riding perhaps, and your mother can be my charming hostess,' he said, smiling at June. 'John Miller has been urging me to sell Ikawa to him for the past two years. He'll be delighted when I tell him my decision.'

'That will mean a vacancy for the post of medical consultant at Kyruba if John Miller moves to Ikawa, won't it?' said Kate. Certain mysterious conversations which she had heard recently were now beginning to make sense.

'Of course. I'm hoping Richard will apply,' said Dr Clark. 'There'll be strong competition, but he's definitely the man for the job.'

'I see,' said Kate quietly.

'I should like to meet this Richard,' said David. 'Where did he train?'

'Oh, he's much older than you,' said Kate, 'You won't have met him.'

'What Kate means is that he's an ancient thirty-two years old,' said Dr Clark laughingly. 'Not a youngster like you, David. When did you finish your year as a house surgeon?'

'Last week,' said David defensively, 'I've joined my father in the family practice. Kate will be able to help us when she returns from Matala in October.'

'So you've got a ready-made job when you come back here?' said Dr Clark to Kate.

'So it would seem,' said Kate quietly. Her mother looked across the table and was surprised at the look of panic in her daughter's eyes.

'I'm sure it will be very interesting,' said June soothingly. 'You'll meet all your old friends.'

'Fascinating,' breathed Kate. Suddenly the family dinner was becoming oppressive. Everyone seemed to be looking at her. She longed to escape. 'Do you mind if I skip the dessert. I'm feeling rather tired.'

'Why of course, my dear,' said June. 'You must be exhausted after your long journey. Have a good sleep and we'll see you in the morning.'

Kate kissed her mother and grandmother and left the room. David followed her out into the hall.

'I think you might have made an effort to stay awake on your first night back,' he said, as soon as they were out of earshot. 'I was hoping we could spend some time alone.'

'I'm sorry, David, I'm absolutely tired out. You go back and finish your dinner. I'll see you tomorrow.'

'I'll pick you up about ten. We'll drive out somewhere and go for a long walk.'

'Lovely. Goodnight, David.'

David held her closely and pressed his mouth hard against her lips. She tried to respond, but without success. David released his grip and looked at her quizzically. 'Have a good sleep,' he said. 'I hope you'll feel better in the morning.'

'I'm sure I will,' said Kate. She turned and went thankfully up to her bedroom. As she closed the door she leaned back against it and breathed a sigh of relief. It was peaceful in her little room with its white walls, pink carpet and marble wash-stand. Everything was just as she remembered as a child. Here at least she felt safe. It was lovely to be home, but how she missed Matala.

CHAPTER EIGHT

DAVID arrived at the farm at ten o'clock next morning, as he had promised.

'Coffee, David?' said June as Mrs Barnes showed him into the breakfast room. 'We're all rather late this morning, I'm afraid. Been having a lazy breakfast.' She picked up the coffee pot and reached for a cup and saucer.

'No thanks, Mrs Mathews. My father has asked me to take Kate back to the surgery, to see the new wing we're building, so I think we should be going. I'm hoping to take Kate to Malham afterwards.'

'That will be nice. Kate will be down in a minute. I took her breakfast in bed. I thought she needed a lie-in, she seemed so tired yesterday.'

David frowned. 'You spoil her, Mrs Mathews. She'll have to learn to look after herself soon.'

'Today is an exception. She had a long journey yesterday, and I think she's been working too hard,' said June lightly. 'Ah, here she comes.'

Kate was still looking rather tired. David kissed her on the cheek. 'Come on; I think it's fresh air you need, my girl. Would you like to go over to Malham?'

'Yes, that would be fun,' said Kate. 'Shall I take my boots with me?'

'I think you'd better. It's sure to be muddy,' said David, pleased at Kate's first show of enthusiasm.

'What about food?' said June.

'That's taken care of, thank you,' said David. 'Mother's packing us a picnic. We've got to call back for it, after we've seen the new surgery.'

'What new surgery?' asked Kate.

'I told you about it in a letter, but I expect you've forgotten,' said David. 'We're having a whole new wing built on. You're going to love working there.'

'Am I? You know, I get the feeling you're trying to sell me something, David,' said Kate.

'Don't be silly,' said June quickly. 'Really, Kate, I think the hot climate has affected your manners. Now hurry along, don't keep David waiting.'

They drove off down the valley to the nearby village and stopped outside the surgery. Inside, David's father was preparing to go off on his morning calls. He greeted Kate warmly.

'I'm glad David has managed to bring you down here at last. He was going to go off for the day without letting me see you. How are you enjoying nursing in the tropics, my dear?'

'Very much, although I haven't had much experience of real tropical nursing, so far. That's why I 'm going to go back until October.'

'So you're going back? Well, we'll just have to find someone to help us until you return. David led me to believe that you were available now.'

David looked annoyed at this. 'I thought she would be, Father. Anyway, I'm still hoping to persuade her to stay,' he added.

David's father smiled, 'If I know Kate, she'll make her own mind up. You'll have difficulty in getting her to change it. Besides, if she's enjoying life in the tropics, she should make the most of it. I wish I'd travelled a bit more when I was young.'

'That's not the point,' said David. 'As my future wife I think she should be settling down.'

'Plenty of time to settle down after you're married,' said Dr Murray. 'A whole lifetime, in fact. I should like to have you here to help us now, Kate, but there's really no problem about trained staff around here. I'll ring the agency when I get back from my rounds. Come and see the new wing.'

Dr Murray showed Kate proudly round the extension which the builders were erecting at the side of the surgery. It was certainly going to be a big improvement on the existing premises, which had changed very little from when Kate was a child.

'David persuaded me it was time we moved with the times and got some new equipment, and everything just snowballed.'

'It's going to be very impressive,' said Kate. 'You'll have no problem finding someone to work here.'

'Yes, but do *you* want to work here?' persisted David.

'Stop pushing her, David,' said his father amiably. 'Give her time.' He smiled at Kate and said, 'David still treats you like a kid sister. Don't let him boss you around.'

'Oh, I'm not going to,' said Kate.

'Good for you,' said Dr Murray. 'Now be off with you. Mother's waiting at home with a picnic basket. She's dying to see you again, Kate.' He kissed her lightly on the cheek and picked up his bag. 'Have a good day, and David . . . take care of her.'

'I will,' David smiled at his father.

They drove on for about half a mile until they came to a large stone-built house, set back from the road. Hollyhocks and roses grew round the front door. Kate followed David into the house. His mother came into the hall and embraced Kate. 'My dear, it's so good to see you back again. Come and have some coffee.' She led them into the sitting-room which faced the steep hillside, with its limestone rocks, boulders, and a stream trickling down to join the river. It was an impressive view. Kate went over to the window.

'I used to love this room when I was a child,' she said. 'Probably because I felt so grown-up when I was in here. Mostly we had to play in the kitchen; do you remember, David?'

David nodded. 'You were such a messy child,' he said. 'Always getting paint all over yourself.'

'Oh, David, she wasn't,' laughed Mrs Murray. 'She was absolutely delightful; hasn't changed as far as I can see,' she added. 'Where are you two going off to today?'

'I thought we'd go over to Malham and climb Gordale Scar,' said David.

'Do be careful, David. It's very slippy at this time of year,' said Mrs Murray.

'I know,' he said. 'But we've climbed it often enough, haven't we Kate? Not likely to hurt ourselves now.'

'Well, I've prepared a picnic basket for you.'

'A basket's no good, Mother. Can't you put it all in my rucksack?'

'David, it's sure to get squashed.'

'No, it won't. Be a dear and transfer it, will you?'

'I'll help you,' said Kate quickly, and the two women went into the kitchen.

'He doesn't change, does he?' said Mrs Murray when they were alone. 'Still as bossy as ever. I sometimes think I must have spoiled him.'

'You've been the perfect mother,' said Kate. 'Don't worry; I can handle David.'

'I hope so, my dear, otherwise you're in for a difficult

time when you're married. Have you two discussed a wedding date yet?'

'Not yet. There's plenty of time. We'll get Mummy's wedding over with first.'

'I'm so looking forward to it,' said Mrs Murray. 'Isn't it marvellous for her, after all these years of being alone. George and I were so thrilled when she told us.'

When the rucksack had been packed, David and Kate said goodbye to Mrs Murray and drove off over the fell to Malham. The road was narrow and winding with limestone walls on either side, and breathtaking views around every corner. Kate began to relax at last as she enjoyed the scenery.

They parked the car at the farm near Gordale Scar and walked along through the fields. The watercress beds in the stream looked fresh and inviting. Kate waded in and picked some to eat later with their picnic. David smiled at her.

'You never could resist the water. It was always my fault if I took you home wet-through. They said I should have looked after you, but you're quite a handful.'

'I know,' Kate laughed happily. 'But you love taking care of me, don't you, David?'

'Of course I do. I can't wait to have you all to myself. Completely mine and mine alone,' he said possessively.

'Don't you think that's a bit old-fashioned,' said Kate. 'I mean, I hope you're not going to stop me having friends of my own.'

'Of course not, but you'll belong to me entirely.' He took her in his arms and pressed his lips savagely against hers.

'David, stop.' Kate struggled to free herself.

'For God's sake, Kate. I've hardly touched you since you got back. What's the matter with you?'

'I'm tired, I'm not in the mood. Let's enjoy our walk. I love this place; don't spoil it for me.'

They walked round the corner of the steep cliff, and came upon the impressive sight of the Gordale Scar waterfall tumbling down the rocks.

'I always think this bit is so marvellous,' said Kate, as she stood, taking in the awe-inspiring scene. 'It's this sort of country that I miss so much when I'm in Africa.'

'I hope that's not all you miss,' said David, as he helped Kate up the first stage of the climb. She squeezed his hand reassuringly.

They climbed in silence, concentrating on finding firm footholds, and trying not to get too wet with the spray from the waterfall, which tumbled down beside them. It was hard work and Kate felt very tired when they reached the top. She flung herself down on to the grass.

'Phew, what a climb! I'd forgotten how tough it was,' she said.

'You're just getting old,' David laughed, 'And you're out of practice. When we're married we'll make time for lots of walks, and keep you fit.'

'Walks! This isn't a walk; its an assault course. I'm terribly thirsty. Can I have a drink, David? There's a thermos of coffee in your rucksack.'

David removed the rucksack from his back and poured out two cups of coffee. They leaned back against a boulder and admired the view as they drank it. David put his arm around Kate's shoulder, but did not attempt to hold her close. Kate relaxed against him, enjoying a feeling of warm companionship. After a few minutes David put the thermos flask away and they started to walk again.

After following the stream to the top of the hill, they

took the path across to Malham Tarn. The morning haze had cleared by this time and the sun glinted on the water. Kate and David stretched out on the grass and enjoyed the warm rays of the sun.

'Shall we have our picnic here?' said Kate, hopefully.

'No, let's press on till we get to Malham Cove,' David was on his feet again. 'Only another mile or so,' he added encouragingly.

Kate stood up and smiled at him. 'David Murray, you're a positive slave-driver.'

He laughed and kissed her lightly on the lips. 'And you're my willing slave,' he murmured.

'Don't you be too sure,' said Kate.

They walked off hand in hand towards the top of Malham Cove which was just visible in the distance. Soon they reached the huge limestone rocks which looked like a giant causeway shining in the warm sunlight.

David found a comfortable grassy place amongst the rocks, and took the food out of his rucksack. It was a perfect spot for a picnic; they were surrounded by impressive boulders and had a magnificent view of the valley far below them.

When they had finished lunch they lay back on the warm grass. David reached for Kate's hand and they remained quiet and contented for a few minutes. Kate felt herself falling asleep, but was suddenly wide awake as David leaned across her. His mouth came down upon hers, heavy and demanding. She felt the weight of his body crushing her.

'David,' she gasped as she tried to escape from beneath him. 'You're hurting me.'

She struggled to free herself, but David pinned her down and started to tear at the buttons of her shirt. His hands were forcing their way inside her bra. In desperation he ripped the thin cotton as he reached for her firm young breasts.

'It's time you started to behave like my wife,' he muttered savagely. 'I'm sick of waiting around for you . . .'

'I'm not your wife,' screamed Kate. 'Stop it David, let me go.'

But David seemed oblivious of everything. Gathering all the strength she could muster, Kate hit him hard in the face. It seemed to bring him to his senses, and he released his grip.

She leapt to her feet and fled along the top of the cove, leaping from boulder to boulder, until she finally flung herself down into a grassy hollow and sobbed uncontrollably.

Some time later she became aware that David was standing on a rock staring down at her as she crouched terrified and trembling. She tried to cover her breasts with her arms. David climbed down into the hollow; Kate screamed as he approached her, but he spoke to her in a soothing voice.

'Darling, I'm sorry. I really don't know what came over me. I've been wanting to make love to you for so long. Something just snapped inside me. I thought that if I could rouse you everything would be all right. Please, please forgive me. I never wanted to hurt you.' He reached out his hand towards her, but she recoiled from him.

'Don't touch me,' she hissed. 'I hate you.'

'Kate, please listen to me. This will never happen again, I promise you. I'll always be gentle with you. I can wait until our wedding night; Is that what you want?' he said, anxiously.

'I don't know what I want, at this moment,' she muttered angrily. 'Pass me my shirt.'

'I'm sorry, darling. It's rather torn, I don't think you can go home in it. I've got your spare sweater somewhere in my rucksack,' he fumbled in his bag, trying to be as helpful as possible. 'Here you are, my darling, put this on; let me help you.'

Kate shrank back once more. 'I can manage,' she said, as she turned her back on him. All trace of their pleasant companionship had gone. David poured the last of the coffee into a cup and held it to Kate's lips.

'Here, drink this; it'll make you feel better.'

Kate sipped obediently at the lukewarm liquid, and began to feel a little better. 'David, I don't think I can ever forget this. I've never seen you like that before.'

'Please try to forget it Kate. I can never forgive myself. I love you so much.'

'Take me home, David. I feel exhausted.'

'Of course you do, my darling. I'll go and get the car and bring it round to the road over there. Wait here for me; I should only be about an hour, if I hurry.'

He started down the side of Malham Cove and soon Kate could see him in the valley below, running along the path at the side of the stream. She watched him until he reached the road back to Gordale Scar and went out of sight. The sun continued to shine down on the top of the Cove, but Kate found she was shivering. Her trust in David had been shattered in five brief minutes. She closed her eyes and tried to put it out of her mind, turning her face towards the warm rays of the sun.

When David arrived she was almost asleep; he roused her gently and helped her across the path to the waiting car. When they reached home, Kate found herself hoping that her mother would be out. She simply wanted to

creep upstairs without anyone seeing her, but as she got out of the car, June Mathews saw her from the window and came out.

'Hello, darling. Had a good day? Goodness, whatever happened to you?'

'I slipped off one of the rocks on the top of Malham Cove, and hurt myself.'

'Oh you poor dear. No bones broken, I hope.'

'No, I had my doctor with me, which was useful,' Kate managed a forced smile. 'I just want to have a bath and change my clothes, so I'll say goodbye, David.'

'You'll come in for a cup of tea?' said June.

'No I'd rather not,' said David quickly. 'I've promised to help Father with evening surgery.' He started the car and drove off down the hill.

June followed Kate upstairs. 'You two haven't quarrelled, have you?' she asked anxiously. 'David seemed very strange just now.'

'Of course not, Mummy,' said Kate as she hurried into the bathroom and locked the door.

'Would you like a cup of tea, darling,' said June from the other side of the door, but Kate had turned the taps full on to cover the sound of her renewed sobbing. June waited anxiously on the landing for a little while, before deciding that her daughter wanted to be left alone.

Kate soaked away some of her misery in her hot bath. Afterwards after putting on one of her prettiest dresses and some of her most expensive French perfume, she began to feel that she would be able to face the family. She found everyone sitting on the terrace outside the sitting-room. Dr Clark came over to greet her as she joined them.

'Sorry to hear about your fall, my dear. Still you were in the right hands. I'm sure David was a great help.'

'Oh yes, he was,' Kate said brightly.

'I'm sure you could do with a drink. What's it to be; gin and tonic?' he said.

'Thank you.' Kate sat down next to her grandmother, who smiled and patted her hand.

'I expect you were rushing along too quickly when you fell,' she said. 'I've always told you, more haste, less speed.'

'No, the rocks are very slippy up there,' said Dr Clark. 'I've only done that walk once, but it can be very tricky.' He handed Kate her drink. 'Here's to a quick recovery.' He was watching her intently, and Kate felt that he was not entirely ignorant of the situation.

'Oh by the way,' he continued. 'I rang Kyruba hospital today. I thought it was about time I told John Miller of my decision to retire. He was working on a case so his secretary said she would get him to phone me this evening. I'm sure he'll be delighted.'

'I hope so,' said June, 'otherwise you're going to have to find someone else.'

'No problem,' said Dr Clark. 'It's a thriving nursing home. Anyway, I'm sure John will want it. Isn't this a marvellous view? So peaceful. I think England is the best place on earth when we have warm, sunny weather. It beats the tropics.'

'Oh, do you think so?' said Kate. 'I love the tropics.'

'So you're looking forward to going back?' he said.

'Very much.'

'But you've only just arrived, darling,' said June. 'You are going to stay for the wedding, next week, I hope?'

Kate laughed, 'Of course, I am, Mummy. I love being at home with you.'

Dr Clark was busily serving more drinks when the phone rang.

'Kate, will you get that for me. It's probably John Miller.'

'Of course.' Kate went inside and picked up the phone. A deep familiar voice said,

'Hello; this is Richard Brooks. May I speak to Dr Clark?'

Kate was taken utterly by surprise. The sound of his voice had a paralysing effect on her. It was several seconds before she was able to reply. 'Richard, this is Kate.'

'Hello, Kate. May I speak to Dr Clark?' he repeated abruptly.

'Of course.' Kate put the phone on the table, and went out on to the terrace. 'It's Richard for you, James,' she said.

'Richard? Perhaps he's ringing on behalf of John Miller.' Dr Clark went into the house, closing the french windows behind him. It was a full five minutes before he returned and said, 'Richard wants to talk to you, Kate.'

'To me? What about?'

'He'll explain everything,' he said mysteriously.

Kate went back to the phone, her heart beating wildly. 'This is Kate,' she said quietly.

'Kate, I'm sorry if I seemed rude just now. I had to clear things with Dr Clark first. The fact of the matter is that Julie refuses to work with Liz any more—I can't think why. They had an awful row today and Julie wanted to give in her notice. I've persuaded her to take an early home leave and reconsider the situation. I think she's just tired and needs a holiday. Anyway, she's promised to stay until you return, so I was just checking with James that you weren't needed at home. He said I should ask you.'

Kate was silent for a moment. 'Yes, that will be

perfectly all right, Richard,' she said in a matter-of-fact voice. 'I'm sorry to hear about Julie. I do hope she'll return after her home leave. She's an excellent nurse.'

'Yes, I know. I think it's a clash of temperaments really. Liz and Julie just don't seem to be able to work together. Anyway it's a relief to know that you're definitely going to return.'

'I'll come back next Thursday, the day after the wedding,' she said. 'Goodbye, Richard.'

'Goodbye,' he said. 'See you soon.' There was a click at the other end. Kate remained very still, thinking about the news. Richard had actually asked her to return. It was incredible! She went back on to the terrace with a light step, and tried to mask the gaiety she felt inside her.

Dr Clark smiled at her: 'You don't seem too unhappy at the prospect of going back to work next week.'

'She can't wait to get back,' said June. 'Who is this Richard you keep talking about?'

'He's in charge of the nursing home at the moment,' said Dr Clark. 'Brilliant young chap. Very lucky to have him.'

'I see,' said June, and watched her daughter carefully. 'Is he married?'

'No, his wife was killed in a car crash,' said Dr Clark. 'Absolutely tragic it was. He's only just getting over it, I think. She was a lovely girl—looked rather like Kate.'

'Did she, indeed,' said June. 'No wonder he likes having my daughter around.'

'Oh Mum, it's not like that at all,' said Kate quickly. 'You always jump to the wrong conclusions.'

'I'm sorry, darling. I'm an incurable romantic; you know that.' She smiled at Dr Clark, lovingly, and he put his arm round her.

'Your mother sees romance in the most unlikely places,' he smiled. 'Kate's perfectly safe with Richard, my dear. She's a respectable soon-to-be-married lady. Richard may enjoy her working with him, but that's as far as it goes.' He turned to Kate. 'I'm surprised to hear about Julie wanting to leave us. She always seemed such a level-headed girl.'

'She finds it difficult to work with Liz,' said Kate quickly. 'So do I, actually.'

'Oh dear,' said Dr Clark. 'I hope you're not going to let Richard down.'

'Of course not. I can cope with Liz. I think I understand her better than Julie does.'

'I hope so.' said Dr Clark.

The phone rang again. 'That's sure to be John Miller,' he said. 'I'll go.'

He came back several minutes later, beaming all over his face. 'Well that's settled then,' he said, 'John's delighted. I knew he would be. I'll get in touch with my solicitor to finalise the details, as soon as possible.'

'Will he move in to Ikawa?' asked Kate.

'Eventually, yes; when the hospital have appointed a new medical consultant. The post has to be advertised, of course,' said Dr Clark.

'So John and Helen will sell Ogiwa House?' said Kate.

'It looks extremely likely,' he said.

Kate sighed. 'I wish I could afford to buy it,' she said.

'My dear, you wouldn't want to live in Africa permanently, would you?' said her grandmother.

'I might, if I had Ogiwa House,' Kate said.

'Is it still as beautiful as when we lived there?' said her mother.

'It hasn't changed at all,' said Kate. 'I love it.'

June's eyes misted over nostalgically. 'We had some

good times there,' she said, in a husky voice. Dr Clark squeezed her hand.

'The best is yet to come, my dear. You'll love my estate in Scotland.'

June smiled at him, 'I know I will. Goodness me, only one week to the wedding. Kate, can you give me a hand with the wedding presents tomorrow. I thought we could put them on display in the breakfast room, and we must be sure to make a list for the thank you letters. That is, unless you've arranged to go out with David.'

'No, we didn't make any plans today.'

'That's good, because I really do need some help. Then I've got to go over to Leeds for a final fitting for my dress. Would you like to come with me, Kate?'

'Of course, I would,' said Kate, happily. 'That's settled then; we'll make an early start tomorrow.'

After dinner Kate helped Mrs Barnes with the dishes, and then slipped quietly out of the kitchen door to the path leading across the fields. She walked for several minutes until she reached a large rock set into the hillside. This had been her favourite spot as a child. It was still warm from the sunshine of the day, and Kate sat on it, quietly watching the sun go down behind the hill. She knew without a shadow of a doubt what she was going to do. It was a momentous decision to make, but she could put it off no longer. Tomorrow she must find time to see David.

CHAPTER NINE

THE next day dawned clear and bright, with a hint of early-morning mist down by the river. Kate looked at the clock in her bedroom. It was only seven, but she felt wide-awake and anxious to start the day. She must see David before she started the wedding preparations with her mother.

Dressing hastily she went downstairs to the kitchen and made some coffee. She carried it into the breakfast room and opened the windows so that she could breathe in the cool fresh morning air. The sheep on the hillside were moving slowly about, cropping the grass. The peaceful scene contrasted heavily with the turmoil of her thoughts.

'I've made the decision,' Kate told herself. 'Now all I have to do is tell David.' She decided to walk to his house across the fields, it would help to clear her thoughts.

The grass was still wet with dew. When she was almost at the village she sat on a stile in the early morning sun. It was much too early to arrive at David's house and she wanted to be absolutely sure of what she was going to say. When she heard the church clock strike nine she took a deep breath and walked the last few hundred yards.

An ambulance was standing outside the house, but this was not unusual. Dr Murray sometimes treated patients at home. When Kate got nearer, however, she saw that David was climbing into the back of the ambulance. He turned and saw her and immediately came to meet her.

'Kate, where on earth have you been? I've been trying to ring you. Nobody knew where you were.'

'I was out walking,' she said coldly. 'I must see you, David.'

'Not now, Kate,' he said urgently. 'Father's been taken ill. He's had a coronary. We're on our way to the hospital.'

'David, I'm so sorry,' she gasped, 'I'd no idea.'

'No, of course not. Listen, I want you to take morning surgery for us. Explain what's happened and deal with everything you can. If it's something you can't handle, ask them to return this evening—oh, and take care of Mother, she's in a state of shock.' He leapt into the ambulance. Kate just had time to glimpse the white-faced prostrate figure of Dr Murray before the doors were closed, and the ambulance moved off at high speed.

Kate found Mrs Murray sitting in the kitchen, staring wide-eyed out of the window.

'Oh, Kate,' she said. 'Thank goodness you're here.' She reached out her hands and Kate took hold of them.

'They'll do everything they can at the hospital,' she said soothingly. 'Meanwhile, you must take care of yourself. Would you like a cup of tea?'

'Yes I would, Kate. It's such a help having you here.' Mrs Murray began to cry. 'George has never been ill before. He came downstairs for breakfast as usual, and sat at the table. I went into the larder to fetch some eggs and when I came back, I found him lying on the floor. I don't know how I'm going to cope.'

Kate put her arms round the older woman and tried to

comfort her. At that moment the doorbell rang. Kate went to answer it. Her mother was standing on the step. She was surprised to see Kate.

'Where have you sprung from?' she said. 'David phoned you. I came as quickly as I could.'

'I've been out for a walk,' Kate said briefly. 'Mummy, will you take care of Mrs Murray, she's in the kitchen. I've got to do the morning surgery.'

'Yes of course, dear.'

June hurried into the kitchen and Kate was able to walk down the road to the surgery. Several people were waiting already. Most of them had heard that Dr Murray had been taken away in an ambulance, but they were nevertheless hopeful that Kate would be able to help them.

Kate spent the next two hours dealing with minor illnesses, and listening to the patients who simply wanted a sympathetic ear. There were a few cases which she thought David should deal with and she asked these to return for evening surgery.

Some of the patients had known Kate since she was a child and were keen to find out when she was coming back to stay. There were several surgical dressings to do, some stitches to remove and a few repeat medications to dispense. Kate had no time to think about her own problem. When the surgery had been cleared, she rang round the patients who had asked for a home-visit to check that there was nothing that was urgent. When she had finished she closed the surgery and walked back to the Murray's house. There she found the two mothers in the sitting-room. Mrs Murray was looking much better.

'We've just phoned the hospital,' she said. 'George is beginning to respond to treatment.'

'That's good news,' said Kate, as she sank thankfully into a chair.

'Let me get you some coffee, my dear,' said Mrs Murray. 'You must be tired after your long session at the surgery.'

'I'll get it,' June said helpfully, and went out to the kitchen.

'Did you manage to cope with everything?' said Mrs Murray.

'Almost everything,' said Kate. 'There were a few things I'm not qualified to deal with, so some patients will be coming back this evening to see David.'

'You'll make the perfect doctor's wife, my dear,' said Mrs Murray. 'You'll be such a help to David.'

Kate did not answer. She looked out of the window at the scene which had looked so beautiful to her yesterday. Was it only yesterday? It seemed like a million years ago. Her mother returned with the coffee and started talking to Mrs Murray, which was a relief for Kate. As she finished her coffee David arrived home. He came into the sitting-room.

'I'm so glad you could come over, Mrs Mathews, and thank you, Kate, for taking surgery. Father's in an oxygen tent, and he's breathing much better. I think you could go and see him now, Mother, but don't try to talk to him. He must have complete rest.'

'I'll drive you over,' said June.

'That's very kind of you,' said Mrs Murray. 'I expect David wants to get a report from Kate about the morning surgery.' She stood up, 'We'll see you both later.'

The two women went out to the car and David and Kate were left alone. He seemed tired and despondent, so she gave him her report as briefly as possible. When she had finished he said,

'What was it you wanted to see me about earlier?'

'Oh . . .' she paused. 'Nothing. It can wait.'

'That's good, because I want to get off on my rounds. Where's the list?'

'It's in the surgery, with the case notes you'll need.'

'Thanks, Kate. You've been a great help.' He kissed her lightly on the cheek. 'I don't know what I'd do without you, especially now. Will you stay here till Mother gets back?'

'Yes, yes of course,' Kate found herself saying.

He smiled at her. 'I'll see you later then.'

She heard the front door close and the sound of David's car pulling away. She felt trapped in a situation from which there was no escape. How could she possibly tell him of her decision now?

The next few days flew by quickly. Kate visited Dr Murray in hospital and was pleased to find that he was making a good recovery, although still not out of danger. David seemed to rely more and more on her help. He wanted her to be with him every minute of the day. Three days before the wedding, as they were driving back from the hospital, Kate was beginning to feel the strain of his emotional demands on her. Firmly she told him she had to spend the next three days with her own family. Her mother had wanted to postpone the wedding, in view of Dr Murray's illness, but Mrs Murray would not hear of it, and insisted that they go ahead. So Kate told David that she would have no time to spare until after the wedding.

'But, Kate, I'm sure you could spare one evening with me. We'll go out to dinner, just the two of us.'

'No, David. I came home to help Mummy with the wedding, and that's what I'm going to do. I'm sorry, but you'll just have to manage without me.'

'Well, I hope you're not going to go back to Africa as soon as the wedding's over.'

Kate took a deep breath. 'I have to go back. I'm needed out there.'

'But you're needed here. I need you. Doesn't that mean anything to you any more?' he cried angrily. 'How do you suppose I'm going to get through all the work at the surgery, with father ill in hospital?'

'Your father was going to arrange for a temporary nurse from the agency. I understood she was coming in this week.'

'Oh yes, we've got a temporary nurse, Kate, but it won't be like having you around the place.'

'Well Mummy needs me for the next few days,' she said. 'I'll see you at the wedding.'

David stopped the car at Kate's house and she got out. 'Goodbye, David,' she said.

He stared straight ahead and did not speak. Her mother came out of the house. 'Are you coming in for a drink, David?' she called.

He turned immediately and said angrily. 'I think Kate will be too busy to have a drink tonight.' Quickly he let in the clutch and drove off down the hill.

'What was all that about?' said June.

'Oh, he's mad at me because I told him I would be too busy to see him before the wedding.'

'Oh, but Kate, you surely don't think I shall need you every minute of the day. Ring him and tell him you can see him tomorrow.'

'No, mother,' said Kate firmly. 'He's got to get used to being without me.'

June was surprised at the firmness in her daughter's voice.

*   *   *

The wedding day finally arrived; it was a moving service and Kate found herself having to hold back the tears of joy which sprang to her eyes at seeing her mother's obvious happiness. If only she could love David as her mother so clearly loved Dr Clark.

The reception was a happy affair, with lots of champagne. The wedding lunch went off without a hitch. Speeches were made by the bridegroom and the best man, who, despite all his other duties, took the responsibility of looking after the bridesmaids to such an extent that he seemed to monopolise Kate throughout the meal. At the end of the lunch, Kate found David waiting for her in the reception area.

'I presume you've no objection if I drive you home,' he said.

'None at all, in fact, I'd be delighted.'

'Well, that makes a change. I thought you were going to go on avoiding me for the rest of the day.'

'I haven't been avoiding you, David. I couldn't help being paired up with the best man all the time.'

'You didn't seem to mind.'

'Why should I? Oh David, do be reasonable. If you're going to drive me home, let's go.' Kate walked out impatiently and made her way to the car park. David went ahead and opened up the car. They drove out on to the road and set off over the hill towards Kate's home. As they reached the top of the hill David pulled off on to the grassy verge and switched off the engine. He reached for Kate's hand.

'David, we must go back home, now,' said Kate. 'We've invited the guests back to see the wedding presents. I promised Mummy I would be there.'

'But I haven't seen you for days. Kate, please don't go

back to Africa. I need you here.' His voice rose
pleadingly.

'We've been over all this before. I'm going back until
October.'

'But everything is so difficult now that father's ill,' he
continued.

'Have you got a temporary nurse yet?' asked Kate.

'Well yes,' he admitted. 'But it's not . . .'

'Is she fully qualified?'

'Yes she's SRN.'

'Fine. Give her some work to do, and stop moaning.'
Kate surprised herself at the way she was speaking to
him.

'But it's not just the work, Kate. You know that.'

'David, we must go back now,' said Kate. 'Let's
discuss it later.'

He grudgingly started up the car and they drove off.
Many of the guests had arrived before them and Kate
hurried upstairs to change out of her bridesmaid's
dress.

In the early evening, June and James Clark set off on
their honeymoon. There were numerous tin cans and old
boots tied to the bumper of their car. June clung to her
daughter for a few brief seconds before she stepped into
the car.

'Goodbye, darling,' she whispered. 'Take care of
yourself.'

They set off in a shower of confetti and Kate stood on
the steps waving until they were out of sight. As she
turned away David put an arm round her and together
they went inside. Everything now seemed an anti-
climax. The guests began to say goodbye and, little by
little, the house became quiet. Grandmother went upstairs to lie down and grandfather went out for a stroll

across the fields. David and Kate sat in the sitting-room, alone at last.

'I've got to go soon, to take evening surgery,' said David. 'Afterwards, I thought we could go out for a drive somewhere.'

'I'm desperately tired, David,' said Kate. 'I really don't want to go out again tonight.'

'Well, tomorrow then?'

Kate cleared her throat nervously. 'I'm going back to Africa tomorrow.' she said quickly.

'Tomorrow? But you can't be!'

'My flight is already booked. I'm catching the early train in the morning, so you see, I need my sleep tonight.'

David took her in his arms. 'I can see your mind's made up, so I won't try to change it. Can I drive you to the station tomorrow?'

'No, grandfather said he would take me. Besides, I expect you'll be busy in the morning. But David, there is something I must tell you before I go . . .'

He looked alarmed at the tone of her voice. 'I don't want to hear it Kate,' he said firmly. 'I've sensed a change in your feelings towards me, but I know it's only temporary. Don't say anything more tonight.' He kissed her lightly on the cheek. 'Goodbye, Kate,' then turning resolutely he strode out of the house. Kate heard the front door close behind him. She was beginning to walk upstairs when the phone rang, so she returned to the sitting-room.

'Hello, Kate Mathews here,' she said.

'Kate, this is Richard.'

'Richard? I'm afraid Dr Clark's just left.'

'No, it's you I wanted.' There was a pause. 'I'm just checking that you're coming out tomorrow.'

'Yes. I shall arrive at the usual time.'

'I expect you'd like someone to meet you at the airport.'

'That would be nice, otherwise I'll take a taxi.'

'No, I'll send Buba . . . or I might come myself if I'm not too busy. Goodnight, Kate.'

'Goodnight, Richard.' Kate put the phone down, and went upstairs. Her heart was beating wildly. She packed her suitcase and had a bath. Then she lay down on her bed and tried to sleep, but it was the early hours of morning before she succeeded.

CHAPTER TEN

IKEJA airport was unbearably hot as Kate battled her way through Customs and Immigration. The journey had seemed interminable, but now that the end was in sight she felt a wave of excitement passing over her. She held her breath as she went out through the wide glass doors which led on to the roadway. The familiar car from the nursing home was parked by the kerb, but it was Buba who was sitting at the wheel. Her spirits sank, but almost immediately she heard a welcome cry as Julie got out of the back of the car and came running to meet her.

'Kate! How lovely to see you again, I've missed you so much.' She flung her arms around Kate and hugged her happily. Buba came across to pick up the luggage.

'Welcome home, Madam,' he said.

Suddenly Kate felt happy to be back. 'It's good of you to meet me, Julie,' she said. 'Who's holding the fort?'

'Madame Liz of course—about time she did some work, for a change,' she laughed. 'Oh, it's so good to see you. Richard was going to come, but he's had to go to Kyruba hospital to see John Miller—something about a job, I think.'

'Oh really?' Kate tried to make her voice sound light. 'What's all this about a row between you and Liz?'

'Oh that? It was hilarious!' Julie started to laugh as they climbed into the car, and set off along the road to Ikawa. 'I simply told Liz I just didn't know how she had ever qualified as a nurse. Honestly she's absolutely clueless! You wouldn't believe how little she knows. She

113

just wanders around in a dream, half the time—dreaming about Richard, mostly. Anyway, she took exception to what I said and went off to tell Richard all about it. He called me into the office and told me I should be more helpful to Liz. *More helpful to Liz!*' Julie's voice rose to a shriek.

'So what did you say to that?' asked Kate.

'I told him that I was tired of playing nursemaid, whereupon he suggested I take early home leave, because I was obviously over-tired.'

'I see. But I thought you had threatened to resign.'

'Oh no. Whatever gave you that idea? I wouldn't do that. No, Richard suggested we make sure you returned, and then I could go home for two months. I'm really looking forward to it. Can't believe my luck.'

Kate was silent as she tried to understand what had really happened.

Julie cut in on her thoughts. 'Well, don't you think I'm a lucky girl?'

'Mm, I do indeed,' said Kate.

'I hope you don't mind coming back so soon?' said Julie anxiously. 'I know you wanted to finish your contract.'

'No, of course I don't mind. Anyway, the wedding's over and Mummy's gone off on her honeymoon. It's all a bit of an anti-climax really.'

'And how's your gorgeous fiancé?'

'He's quite well considering his father had a coronary last week. It's been rather distressing for all of us.'

'I'm sorry to hear that. Will his father be all right?'

'Yes, he's out of danger now. David's had to take over the family practice.'

'I'm surprised he let you return.'

'He wasn't too keen on it, but I felt I had to finish what

I started to do.' There was a firmness in Kate's voice.

'You're a tough character when you need to be,' said Julie, and squeezed Kate's hand. 'Well, I'm glad you're back. I only hope you have more success with Madame Liz than I have. You'll just have to be as hard as nails with her.'

Kate laughed. 'I intend to be. When are you going home?'

'Tomorrow,' said Julie happily.

'You haven't wasted much time.'

'No. I made a provisional booking and confirmed it when I knew you were definitely going to arrive.'

The car went through the gates and pulled up in front of the nursing home. Buba got out and opened the doors for them, before busying himself with the luggage. As they started to walk up the steps, Liz came out on to the verandah, looking impeccably cool and sophisticated in her white uniform, in spite of the intense heat.

'Ah, there you are,' she said, walking languidly towards them. 'I was just hoping I might take a break for some tea. I've been run off my feet all afternoon.'

'I can't imagine how six patients could possibly run you off your feet,' said Julie acidly. 'Go and have your tea. I'll take over for a while. See you later, Kate.' She went off towards the patients' wing.

Kate followed Buba, as he took the luggage to her room. Liz was already calling Musa to serve tea, and had settled herself in a comfortable chair on the verandah.

It was good to be back in her little room. The first thing Kate noticed was a bowl of expensive-looking flowers on her dressing table with a simple card which said 'Welcome back to Ikawa'. There was no signature, and the card was typewritten. Her heart began to beat rapidly. She undressed and stood under the shower for several minutes. Then she lay full-length on her bed feeling relaxed and refreshed again. Her bedside phone rang.

'Hello, Kate Mathews here.'

'Kate, it's Mike,' said the deep masculine voice at the other end. 'Welcome back. Did you get my flowers?'

'Oh . . . yes. Thank you Mike; what a lovely thought. They're beautiful.'

'Did you have a good holiday?' he continued.

'Yes, very pleasant. The wedding went off well, and it was lovely to see all my family.'

'Good. I was wondering if you'd like to go out tonight.'

'Tonight? Oh not tonight, Mike. I'm absolutely tired out. I've been travelling since early morning, you know.'

'Well tomorrow then?' he persisted.

'Er . . . tomorrow; unless I'm needed here, that should be OK. What did you have in mind?'

'Well, I thought a spot of dinner at the Country Club and then a look at the night spots of Kyruba.'

'Sounds fun. I'll ring you tomorrow as soon as I know the duty schedule.'

'OK, look forward to hearing from you. 'Bye, Kate.'

'Goodbye, Mike.' She put the phone down and started to unpack. When everything was neatly hung or put away, she dressed in one of the new dresses she had bought while shopping with her mother. It was in cool white cotton, with a deep neckline and a full skirt. She had chosen it with great care, because now she knew exactly the sort of clothes which looked good on her, for the tropical evenings. She went across the garden to the verandah where Liz was still sitting drinking tea.

'That's a rather nice dress,' said Liz as Kate joined her. 'You must have done some shopping while you were in England.'

'Yes, I managed to spend a day in Leeds with my mother,' said Kate, as she sat down next to Liz.

'I'm dying to get back to civilisation again; I haven't got a thing to wear,' Liz moaned.

'I thought you'd brought plenty of clothes with you,' said Kate.

'Oh yes, but they're all the wrong kind. I didn't realise everything was going to be so primitive out here.' She sighed wearily. 'I'm afraid the tea's not fit to drink. You'll have to get Musa to make you some fresh.'

Musa, hovering in the background, came out on to the verandah and stood by Kate's chair enquiringly.

'Madam?' he said smiling.

Kate was about to ask for some more tea, when she saw Richard striding out through the french doors. The colour rose to her cheeks as he came towards her and took her hand.

'Thanks for coming back so soon, Kate,' he said warmly.

'I was just going to order some fresh tea,' said Kate, to cover her confusion. 'Would you like some?'

'Tea? Good heavens, we need something stronger to celebrate your return. Bring the champagne from the fridge, Musa.'

'Champagne? My, we are being spoilt,' said Liz.

'Don't worry, it won't last,' said Richard. 'I shall crack my whip in the morning and you'll both have to jump to it.'

Liz groaned. 'This place is full of slave drivers,' she said to Kate.

'Well, what did you expect? A holiday camp?' Richard said. 'We work hard and play hard, isn't that right, Kate?'

'If you say so,' said Kate quietly.

'Is the pep-talk over yet?' said Liz. 'I've worked very hard today, so I presume I now qualify for a little pleasure.' She smiled at Richard. 'What have you planned for this evening?'

'Planned? Nothing much. A glass of champagne, dinner in the company of three beautiful ladies . . .'

'I'm glad you said *three* ladies,' said Julie, coming out on to the verandah. 'I was beginning to think I was excluded from all the fun. I hope the champagne isn't to celebrate my departure.'

Musa appeared with the bottle and some glasses. Richard expertly removed the cork and poured the champagne.

'Welcome back, Kate,' he said as he touched his glass to hers. Their eyes met for one brief second before Kate turned away. She was aware that Liz was watching them carefully.

'I hope I get the same VIP treatment when I return,' said Julie.

'Oh, you will Julie, I promise you,' said Richard amiably.

The four of them sat on the verandah drinking the champagne. There was a pleasant feeling of companionship. Kate began to feel perhaps life was going to run smoothly at Ikawa after all. It was Liz who shattered the peace.

'So we're all going to spend the evening stuck out here then. Seems rather a waste,' she said petulantly.

'Oh I don't know,' said Richard quietly. 'What would you prefer to do?'

'I thought perhaps we could go down to Kyruba or something.'

'No, not tonight,' he said evenly. 'Perhaps tomorrow.'

'Oh Richard, that reminds me,' said Kate quickly. 'Mike Gregson just rang me. He wants to take me out tomorrow night. Will that be all right?'

'Mike Gregson rang?' said Richard. 'He hasn't wasted much time. Well I suppose it will have to be OK,' he said irritably.

'But that means I shall have to stay here tomorrow night,' said Liz.

'It won't kill you,' said Richard. 'I'll stay here with you. Perhaps we'll open another bottle of champagne, when we've settled the patients.' He smiled at Liz and she seemed happy again. Richard lifted up the bottle. 'Have some more champagne, Liz.'

Liz held out her glass and Richard poured the rest of the champagne into it. 'That seems to be the end of that bottle, ladies. Remind me to put one in the fridge for tomorrow, Liz.' He drained his glass and stood up. 'I'd better go and see what's happening to the patients. See you all at dinner.'

With that he strode purposefully across the verandah towards the patients' wing.

'I must go and pack,' said Julie.

'I hope you enjoy your holiday,' said Liz. 'I expect the change will do you good.'

'I expect it will,' said Julie, as she started off across the garden.

'I'll come with you,' said Kate. 'You might need some help.

They made their way into Julie's room. 'Sit down,' said Julie. 'I've almost finished. There's nothing you can do, but I'm so glad you came over with me. It gives us a chance to talk. Now you can see what I've had to put up with. Those two have been going out and leaving me as often as they possibly could. It's always Liz who suggests it, and Richard just seems as if he can't say no. I think she's bewitched him.'

Kate laughed. 'Oh Julie, you do exaggerate. I'm sure there's nothing in it.'

'Don't you be too sure. She's besotted with him and quite determined to get him. When a girl like that sets out to capture someone . . .'

'You're far too dramatic,' Kate broke in. 'I think they're just good friends.'

'Think what you like,' Julie shut the case with a bang, and sat on top of it, as she struggled with the clasps. 'Anyway, I'm glad you're going out tomorrow. It's about time Liz had to stay behind.'

The rest of the evening passed without any further tension. They all made polite conversation at the dinner table, and then Julie and Kate went to bed early, leaving Liz and Richard on the verandah together.

Next day after saying goodbye to Julie, Kate made her way to the patients' wing. She made a check on the case notes and set out the medicine tray with the required drugs. There had been a number of changes while she was away. Mr Brown, the psoriasis case was back, so she called in to see him first. He was delighted to see her.

'Nurse Mathews, how lovely to see you. I thought you'd deserted us.'

'I wouldn't do that, Mr Brown. You know how I miss all of you.' Kate smiled at him. 'I see we're going to change your medication.'

'I hope so, Nurse. I've put on so much weight. These wonder drugs cure one bad thing only to cause another.'

'Yes, but your skin seems to be improving,' she said,

running her fingers expertly over the back of his hand. She noted the bloated appearance of the flesh under the skin. 'I think we'll be able to get rid of this extra weight.' she said. 'You'll just have to be patient.'

'If you're here, Nurse, I'll be as patient as you like,' he said, smiling through his swollen face. Kate dispensed the necessary drugs and watched while he took them.

'I'll be along to apply your ointment as soon as I can,' she said. 'Have you everything you need?'

'Yes thanks, Nurse. I've got everything I need, now that you're back.'

'Flattery will get you nowhere,' said Kate with mock severity. 'I'll see you later.' She closed the door behind her and went into the next room to deal with Mrs Marshall.

Mrs Marshall had returned while Kate was away, complaining of severe nervous exhaustion. She had spent three weeks at home and it had all been too much for her. 'I can't go on,' she complained, as Kate came through the door. 'Nobody can do anything for me. It's a waste of time and money staying here.'

'Then why did you come back?' said Kate.

'Where else could I go? Not to the hospital, that's for sure. It's a perfectly dreadful place—no privacy.'

'I wonder if we should get a second opinion,' said Kate, thoughtfully.

'Second opinion?' Mrs Marshall brightened visibly. 'Yes, why not, indeed, Dr Brooks hasn't been able to cure me.'

'I don't think anyone can cure you Mrs Marshall, until we find out what's wrong with you,' said Kate quietly. 'Perhaps we could call in Dr Stewart from Kyruba Hospital, to give us his opinion.'

'Dr Stewart?' said Mrs Marshall 'And what can he do?'

'Well, he's a consultant psychiatrist . . .'

'A psychiatrist? So you think I'm mad?' she shrieked.

'No, no of course not Mrs Marshall,' said Kate soothingly. 'I merely think it would be a good idea to have a second opinion.'

Mrs Marshall sank back against her pillows and started to cry loudly. The door opened and Richard came in,

'What on earth's going on, Nurse Mathews,' he said severely. 'I could hear the noise all the way down the corridor.'

'Nurse Mathews thinks I'm mad,' howled Mrs Marshall. 'She wants me to see a psychiatrist.'

'Is this true, Nurse?' said Richard.

'Of course I don't think Mrs Marshall is mad, but I do think it wouldn't do any harm to have a second opinion about her recurrent nervous exhaustion.'

'Don't you think decisions of that kind are my affair,' he said coldly, then remembering that the patient was listening, he put on his most charming bedside manner.

'There, there Mrs Marshall. A little misunderstanding. Nurse was only trying to be helpful.' He took a tissue from the box at the side of the bed and wiped her eyes. 'We'll soon have you better,' he said soothingly.

Mrs Marshall was enjoying the extra fuss and attention. 'Perhaps it would be a good idea if I see a psychiatrist,' she said, smiling weakly. 'I think a second opinion might be a good idea.'

'I'll see what I can do,' said Richard. He turned towards Kate. 'Would you come along to my office, Nurse, when you've given Mrs Marshall her medication.'

'Certainly Dr Brooks.' Kate said, outwardly calm but inwardly seething with indignation. When Richard had gone, Kate settled Mrs Marshall, promising to return again as soon as she had time.

Richard was sitting at the desk in his office. He kept her waiting a full five minutes while he carried on writing. When he finally looked up his eyes were cold and stern.

'How dare you take it on yourself to suggest the treatment required by a patient,' he said severely. 'I am in charge here. You should have consulted me first.'

'I'm sorry, but we don't seem to be making any progress with Mrs Marshall and I thought a second opinion might be helpful. I realise now that I shouldn't have mentioned it to Mrs Marshall before discussing it with you, but I wish you hadn't tried to humiliate me in front of a patient.'

Richard's eyes flashed angrily. 'Don't tell me how to behave in front of a patient. You're the one who started all this.' He paused and picked up his pen again. Kate noticed that his fingers were trembling. She went towards the door.

'If you've finished with me, I'll go back to my work,' she said.

'No, I haven't finished with you,' he said severely. 'Come back here.'

She turned at the sound of his voice, but remained by the door.

'Kate . . .' he paused for a few seconds before raising his eyes from the desk.

'Yes?' she said quietly, and their eyes met. For a moment it seemed as if his anger had vanished, then the harsh tone returned.

'I don't think we need to discuss this further,' he said.

'I will arrange for Dr Stewart to visit Mrs Marshall at her request. That will be all.'

Kate turned and went out of the room. The tears were springing to her eyes. As she went down the corridor she almost collided with Liz, who was coming round the corner.

'Hey, steady on,' Liz said. 'Look where you're going. Whatever's the matter?'

'It's nothing,' Kate blew her nose vigorously. 'Just a touch of hay-fever, I think.'

'Strange; I wouldn't have thought you got hay fever out here in the tropics,' said Liz.

'Liz, will you finish the medicines,' said Kate. 'I've got as far as Mr Brown and Mrs Marshall. I must go to my room, but I'll be back soon.'

'Of course,' Liz looked at her quizzically. 'Better get something for your hay fever.'

Kate hurried off to her room and washed her face in cold water. She dabbed her eyes with the towel and then looked at her reflection in the mirror. 'Better wait here for a few minutes,' she thought. 'I won't give him the satisfaction of knowing he's upset me.' She blew her nose again, applied fresh makeup and smiled at herself in the mirror. She looked perfectly composed again. Picking up the phone she dialled the number of Kyruba hospital and asked to speak to Mike Gregson.

'Hello, Mike,' she said, when he arrived.

'Hello, Kate. Are you OK for tonight?'

'Yes. Liz and Richard will be here.'

'That's marvellous. I'll pick you up about eight. Would you like to go to the Country Club?'

'Yes; I've never been there before.'

'Fine. I think you'll enjoy it. I'll book a table. See you later.'

'Goodbye, Mike.' Kate put the phone down and walked across the garden back to the patients' swing. Liz was sitting at the desk in the reception area.

'How's the hay fever?' she asked.

'Much better,' said Kate. 'Did you finish the medicines?'

'Yes. I thought I'd leave the dressings until you came back,' said Liz.

'Well, let's get started shall we,' said Kate briskly.

The day passed quickly and Kate had no time to brood about her clash with Richard. In the evening she went off duty, showered, changed and waited for Mike on the verandah. She had not seen Richard since the morning. Apparently he had spent the day in his office. When she heard the sound of Mike's car in the drive, she stood up to go and meet him.

Richard got there before her and was deep in conversation with Mike when Kate appeared on the steps. The two men looked up at her from the drive. Mike came up the steps to meet her.

'Kate you look wonderful,' he said. 'But then you always do, doesn't she, Richard?'

Richard did not reply. He hurried inside without looking at Kate.

Mike drove off down the drive. 'Did you know Richard was in line for medical consultant at Kyruba?' he asked as they drove away.

'Yes, Dr Clark told me when I was in England,' said Kate.

'He stands a very good chance of getting it,' said Mike. 'Although there's some quite tough opposition. John Miller says the applications are still coming in, and some from quite senior men. I haven't dared to apply.'

'Why not?' said Kate.

'I haven't had enough experience. Besides I'm not such an authoritarian as Richard. He's a born leader, don't you think so?'

'He certainly likes to have his own way,' said Kate.

They drove up to the Ikawa Country Club which was an impressive building standing in its own grounds. The numerous palm trees were lit by carefully concealed lights shining up to the sky so that the effect was a mass of blazing colours. A steward in immaculate white uniform with a red cummerbund round his waist, came down the steps to greet them. He took them into the foyer where another steward showed them to their table. The dining room was in the old colonial style and had maintained the decor of the 1930s. There was no air-conditioning but large electric fans whirred ceaselessly in the ceiling.

'What an interesting place,' said Kate. 'I'm so glad we came here. I remember my father used to talk about it, when I was a child.'

'Oh, it's very pukka,' said Mike. 'Definitely the place to be, especially if you're trying to impress someone.' They both laughed.

'Well, I'm impressed,' she said.

A steward brought them the menu and they ordered. Mike insisted they drank champagne as an apéritif. 'The service is rather slow,' he said, 'So we'll probably finish the bottle before the first course.'

They had a couple of dances before the food arrived.

'What did I tell you,' said Mike. 'You need plenty of time in this place. Don't come here if you're in a hurry.'

As they started eating Kate noticed several Africans coming into the dining room. At the centre of the group was a large wealthy-looking man obviously in charge of the party. Kate recognised him immediately as Chief

Ladipo. As he passed near her table he saw her and came over to shake her by the hand.

'Nurse Mathews; it's good to see you. They told me you'd gone back to England.'

'I went home for a couple of weeks, that's all. You're looking well. How's the leg?'

'Fine. You did a marvellous job for me. Now look here, you promised to come and see me. When are you coming?'

Kate was quite taken aback. 'I don't know when my off-duty . . .' she started to say, but Chief Ladipo interrupted her impatiently.

'Off-duty, off-duty,' he repeated. 'Come and see me on Sunday. Come for the whole day. I'll send my driver for you in the morning about ten. OK?'

'Well I can't promise anything,' she said.

'I'll ring up your chief tomorrow and fix it with him,' he said. 'What's his name? Dr Brooks? Yes I'll ring him tomorrow. Now what are you drinking? Champagne?' He snapped his fingers at the nearest waiter. 'Bring another bottle of champagne for Madam.' He smiled a wide beaming smile at her, showing large white shining teeth. 'See you on Sunday. Bring your friend.' He waved his arm expansively at Mike, then moved on towards his table, entirely surrounded by friends and attentive waiters.

Mike laughed. 'There goes a man who won't take no for an answer.'

'Mike, what am I going to do?'

'Do? Why, you must go of course. He's obviously very rich. You'll have a marvellous time. I'll come with you. Well, he did invite me after all.'

'Liz will be furious,' said Kate.

'What's it got to do with Liz?'

'I don't think she'll enjoy doing all the work on Sunday.'

'She had plenty of off-duty while you were away. Richard was always taking her out,' said Mike.

A waiter arrived with another bottle of champagne. Kate giggled. 'I don't think I can drink anymore,' she said.

'Don't be silly. You haven't started yet.' Mike laughed, as he topped up her glass. They continued to drink champagne, and danced between each course. By the end of the evening they were both feeling very merry.

'I don't know when I've enjoyed myself so much,' said Kate, as they danced the last dance. 'You're a good friend, Mike.'

'Yes, I'm just a good friend,' he said and pulled a wry face.

Kate glanced at him questioningly, but his expression changed back immediately.

'Where shall we go now?' he laughed.

'Now? Don't you think we should be going back?'

'The night is young, and I promised to show you the night spots of Kyruba. Come on let's go.'

'Mike, it's one o'clock.'

'So? Let's make a night of it.' His *joie-de-vivre* was infectious. Kate found herself laughing happily as she climbed into his car. They sped off down the road to Kyruba. Up above them, the moon shone, casting a white glow over the surrounding countryside. The roof of the car was down and a delicious cool breeze blew through Kate's hair.

'This is so exhilarating, Mike.'

'What did I tell you?' he shouted above the noise of the car and the wind. 'I knew you'd enjoy yourself.'

Mike parked the car by the quay-side and they walked along the jetty, staring down into the dark waters of the sea. The ships in the harbour were still, but lights twinkled from the portholes and the sound of music and laughter drifted across the water.

'This is the best time to be in Kyruba,' he said, as he took Kate's arm and steered her along the waterfront. Neon lights flashed the name 'Chez Simon' outside one of the bars.

'Oh, let's go to Chez Simon,' said Kate. 'Liz and Richard spent an evening there.'

'Really? I wouldn't have thought Liz would have approved of a place like this.'

'She didn't,' laughed Kate. 'But I'd still like to see it.'

They climbed the narrow wooden staircase on to the top floor which was mostly open to the stars and the sky. Plants and shrubs were growing in large pots, giving the effect of a tropical garden.

'It's really rather nice here,' said Kate, as the waiter found them a table. 'I can't think why Liz didn't like it.'

'Ah, but she's used to expensive restaurants. I don't think she likes the simple life,' said Mike.

There was a small group of musicians playing African music. They danced several dances before Kate began to feel tired.

'Mike, I really think we ought to go back. I'll never be able to work in the morning, if I don't get some sleep,' she said. 'It's been an absolutely fabulous evening, but I think we should go now.'

'Right, let's go,' said Mike amiably.

When they reached Ikawa, Mike got out of the car to take Kate up the steps. 'Aren't you going to offer me a night cap?' he said.

'Don't you think we've had enough to drink?' giggled Kate. 'I feel as if champagne will be coming out of my ears soon.'

'Well, make some coffee then,' Mike said, and sank down into one of the chairs on the verandah. The chair squeaked loudly and they both laughed.

'Ssh!' said Kate. 'You'll wake everybody up.' She turned to go into the house, and found Richard standing in the doorway.

'What time do you call this?' he said sternly.

'I say old chap, steady on,' said Mike as he swayed to his feet.

'You stay out of this,' snapped Richard. 'You've obviously had a few too many. That's nothing new, but I object to you bringing Kate back in the middle of the night.'

'Mike, I think you'd better go,' said Kate quietly, 'Thank you for a lovely evening.'

For one moment Mike looked as if he was going to challenge Richard, then he thought better of it, and got into his car.

'Goodbye, darling,' he called and blew a kiss to Kate, as he roared off down the drive.

'I suggest you take the morning off tomorrow and catch up on your sleep,' said Richard sternly.

'It's not necessary,' said Kate equally coldly.

'That is an order,' snapped Richard. 'I don't like my staff to be half asleep whilst on duty. You can report to me at midday. Now I suggest you go and get some sleep. I'll see you to your room.'

They walked across the garden in silence. As they reached Kate's room Richard said, 'I hope this sort of thing won't happen again, Kate.'

'What sort of thing?' she said angrily.

'I think you know very well what I mean. I am responsible for you while you're out here and I don't like you staying out half the night with Mike Gregson.'

'Thank you for your concern, Richard, but I can take care of myself. You don't need to worry about me.'

'Oh but I do,' he said quietly. The anger had vanished. She could barely trust herself to speak.

'I'll try to remember,' she said as she turned and went into her room, closing the door quietly behind her.

The delightful evening had suddenly turned sour. How dare Richard treat her like a spoilt child! She tugged at the zip of her dress, and as it cascaded to the floor, the anger subsided into heartbreak, and she leaned against the wall, sobbing uncontrollably. She did not hear the soft tap on the door as Richard returned to apologise for his harshness, and thus, as the door opened, she all but fell into his arms.

Richard was startled to feel the almost naked body as he comforted her, but Kate, inhibitions dulled by the champagne, only wanted to be soothed and loved. Her arms clung round his neck and her lips eagerly sought his, while her body moulded its yielding form to Richard's manly frame. Kate's mind was no longer in control, and at his intimate touch, her whole body exploded into action, striving to assuage that primeval urge. Her tongue darted into his mouth, her arms pulling his head closer, and her melting thighs grasped Richard's leg, thrusting forward with an urgent need.

As though awakening from a dream, Richard started and then gently pushed her from him.

'No, Kate. It can't be like this. You've had too much to drink and you don't know what you're doing.'

Kate gave a groan of frustration and then collapsed into his arms. She had passed out, and therefore did not see the tender look he gave her, as he carried her to her bed, covered her with a sheet, and softly went out, closing the door behind him.

CHAPTER ELEVEN

Kᴀᴛᴇ awoke refreshed from her long sleep. She did not remember much of the previous evening after Chez Simon's, but vaguely remembered seeing Richard. She got up and put on a silk dressing-gown, wondering why she had not fully undressed last night. The morning sun was already high in the sky and her little room felt stifling. She flung open the windows and went out on to the verandah. A long brown lizard scuttled away into the bushes, its bright red head shining in the sunlight. She breathed in the scent of roses from the garden. It felt good to be alive. After a quick shower, she dressed in her uniform and went across the garden to find Musa. Having ordered her coffee she sat on the verandah and waited. There was a rustle of starched apron behind her and Liz appeared.

'So you've managed to drag yourself out of bed at last,' she said. 'I've been on duty for hours.'

Kate smiled at her. 'I'll take over when I've had some coffee.'

'I should hope so. I told Richard, it just isn't fair, making me work so hard.'

Kate did not reply. She accepted the coffee which Musa brought for her. There seemed no point in arguing with Liz.

'Did you have a good time?' asked Liz grudgingly after a while.

'Fabulous,' said Kate. 'We had dinner at the Country

133

Club and then went on to Chez Simon.'

'Chez Simon? That dump?' said Liz.

'I thought it was rather fun,' said Kate smoothly. 'Mike and I had a marvellous time.'

'You're quite keen on Mike aren't you?' said Liz.

'He's a good friend,' said Kate.

'Just a good friend?' repeated Liz.

'Why, of course.' Kate finished her coffee and stood up. 'I'll go and do some work.'

Richard was in his office when Kate tapped lightly on his door. She peeped in round the door. 'I hope we weren't too noisy when we came back last night,' she said. 'I can't really remember much at all.'

Richard seemed slightly embarrassed but said, 'Of course not. Come in, Kate. I hope you feel better after your sleep.'

'I feel fine, thank you.'

'Good, then perhaps you could go round and see if Liz has finished the morning routine. But before you go, there is one more thing . . .' He paused. 'I've just had a phone call from Chief Ladipo.' He frowned.

'Oh yes, I can explain . . .' began Kate, but Richard continued.

'It seems you've arranged to spend the day there on Sunday. Once again, I do wish you'd consulted me.'

'Richard, he wouldn't take no for an answer. I tried to put him off, but he insisted. Look, if it's inconvenient I can . . .'

'No no, that's all right. He's a very influential man around here, used to getting his own way. I told him you could go.'

Kate smiled. 'Thank you, Richard.'

'The only problem is, I shall have to leave Liz in charge,' he continued.

Kate's eyes widened. 'Do you think that's a good idea?' she said.

'No, I don't,' he smiled. 'But I've no option. I've got an appointment at Kyruba hospital in the afternoon, which means I shall have to be away for two or three hours.'

'Liz can ring you if she has a problem,' said Kate.

'I suppose so. Still, I would have preferred you to have been here. Are you looking forward to going?'

'I think it should be a good experience. I've never been to an African palace before.'

'Nor have I. Are you nervous?' he smiled.

'Not really. Mike said he would come with me.'

Richard's expression changed. 'I see. Chief Ladipo didn't mention that.'

'It was a very casual sort of invitation. He's probably forgotten.'

'But Mike won't forget,' he said. 'You will remind him that you have to return in the evening, won't you?'

'Of course,' said Kate. She stood up and went to the door. 'I will be sure to return before my coach changes into a pumpkin.' She grinned mischievously and he smiled back at her.

'Run along with you,' he said.

She went to see Mr Brown.

'Why haven't I had my ointment put on yet?' he demanded, as she went through the door. This was rather abrupt for Mr Brown and Kate looked at him anxiously.

'I'm sorry, Mr Brown. I think Nurse Mason must have forgotten. I'll do it for you now.' She started to scrub her hands at the sink.

'She said she was coming an hour ago, and I've been waiting,' he continued peevishly.

'Never mind, I'm here now,' said Kate soothingly. 'Let's have a look at you.' She examined his skin carefully and then started to apply the soothing ointment.

'Anyway, I'm glad it's you who's doing it, Nurse,' he said. 'Nurse Mason has such awful long nails. She keeps scratching me.'

Kate laughed. 'They're her pride and joy, Mr Brown. We've tried to get her to cut them, but she won't think of it.'

When she had finished she washed her hands thoroughly and then tidied up the room.

'What a mess you're in,' she exclaimed.

'I can't be bothered any more,' he said. 'I'm so fed up.'

Kate was alarmed at his tone. He was usually such a cheerful man. 'What's the trouble?' she asked.

'Oh, I don't know. I just don't seem to be getting any better,' he said.

'Well, give it time,' said Kate. 'This new drug you're on has had some marvellous results. As I said before, you'll just have to be patient. I'll pop back later and we'll have a long chat when I've got more time.'

'Yes, please do,' he said anxiously.

She smiled at him as she went out. 'Poor Mr Brown,' she thought. 'He's been so patient. I'll have to cheer him up.' She went in to see Mrs Marshall who was excited at the prospect of a visit from the eminent Dr Stewart.

'I'm so glad you thought of it, Nurse,' she said. 'I don't mind what it costs, if I can only get my health back again. I've been ill for such a long time.' She sighed wearily. Kate escaped as quickly as she could so that she could deal with the other patients. Most of the morning work had been done but there were several small jobs which Liz had forgotten to do.

Musa arrived with the food trolley and helped Kate to

serve lunch. When they had cleared away, Kate settled the patients for their siesta and went across to the dining room for her own lunch.

Richard and Liz were still sitting at the table.

'Everything OK?' asked Richard.

'More or less,' said Kate. 'I'll go back as soon as I've finished my lunch. Mr Brown seems rather depressed today. I've promised to go and cheer him up.'

'He seemed all right when I saw him,' said Liz.

'How was his skin?' said Kate casually.

'His skin? It seemed OK.'

'Was that why you decided not to apply his ointment?' said Kate.

'I didn't know it needed doing every day,' said Liz defensively. 'I gave him his tablets and I thought that was all that needed doing. How was I to know?'

'You could have looked at his treatment sheet,' said Kate.

'Look girls, let's leave it, shall we,' put in Richard quickly. 'Have your lunch, Kate, and Liz, do try to be more methodical.'

'Oh don't you start,' said Liz. 'I'm going for a nap. This place wears me out.' She got up and left the room.

'I think she'll be all right when she's got into the routine,' said Richard. 'This heat doesn't help either. She's not used to a tropical climate you know.'

'No, of course not,' said Kate quietly. She continued to eat her lunch. Richard remained at the table watching her.

'Do you feel like a swim, this afternoon?' he said suddenly.

Kate looked up, startled. 'I've told you, I've promised to go back to see Mr Brown.'

'But you can't spend all the afternoon with him. I'll meet you by the pool about four. Joseph will be back by then.' He stood up. 'Four o'clock then?'

'You're very persuasive,' she said, smiling. 'I think I shall feel like a swim in a couple of hours.'

'Good. See you later.' He strode out of the dining room and she watched him going towards the patients' wing.

'He must be going to check on Mr Brown for himself,' she thought. She finished her lunch and went back to the patients' wing. Sure enough, she found Richard talking to Mr Brown. He stood up when she came in.

'I've just been telling Mr Brown how confident I am about his treatment. One of the finest drugs we have,' he said. 'Give it time, Mr Brown; you'll have to be patient.'

'That's what nurse keeps telling me,' he said, with a wry grin.

Kate sat down. 'How about a game of Scrabble?' she said, getting the board out.

'Yes, all right,' he said.

'I'll leave you two to your game,' said Richard. 'Don't forget our appointment, Nurse Mathews.'

Kate smiled at him. 'I won't,' she said.

A couple of hours later Joseph arrived on duty, but their game was still unfinished. Kate stood up. 'I'm afraid I'll have to go. Leave the board as it is, and we'll finish it tomorrow.'

He looked at her sadly; 'Do you have to go?' he said pitifully.

'I'm afraid so. I can't spend all my time with you. Haven't you got anything you want to read?'

'Not really,' he looked at the shelf of books near his bed. 'I can't seem to concentrate.'

'I'll pop back later,' Kate promised. She felt guilty as she slipped away across the garden. Richard was already at the pool.

'Come on, slow-coach,' he called.

'I've got to change,' she said, 'I couldn't leave Mr Brown until now.'

'Of course you could. You can't give him all your time. Is Joseph back?'

'Just arrived.'

'Good, well hurry up then.' He dived into the pool and swam easily to the other side.

Kate went to her room and changed into her bikini. As she ran along the side of the pool, Richard splashed water on her.

'Come on, dive in,' he called.

'I can't dive,' she said.

'Jump, then.'

Kate jumped into the pool and started to swim across it. Richard swam by the side of her, trying to get her to improve her stroke.

'You're putting your hands in too shallow,' he called. 'Put them deeper into the water, and you'll go further.'

Kate was so engrossed with trying to change her style that she failed to notice the slim blonde figure in a miniscule white bikini, watching them from the garden. Liz strolled over and called out,

'Can anyone join in the swimming lesson?'

Richard turned and saw her. 'Sure, come on in.'

'No thanks,' she shuddered. 'I don't want to get my new bikini wet. I'll just sit here and watch you. I might learn something.'

She settled herself on a sunbed at the edge of the pool. Kate found it difficult to ignore the piercing blue eyes watching them both eagerly. She swam for a couple of lengths and then climbed out, shaking the water from her.

'That didn't take long,' said Liz. 'Have you learned everything Richard can teach you?'

'No, she hasn't,' said Richard. 'Her stroke is improving but she'll need a lot more practice.'

'And do you think you could teach me?' said Liz in a soft voice.

'Not unless you come into the pool,' he called back.

'OK, I'll go and change.' Liz hurried away and was back in a few minutes, this time in a black bikini, not quite so small as the white one.

'I think this one should be OK,' she said, as she eased herself gently into the water. 'Richard, come here and help me.'

He swam towards her and she put her hands on his shoulders. 'Can you take me across the pool, so that I can get the feel of the water,' she murmured, clinging tightly to him.

'Well, I suppose so, but you'll have to try and swim by yourself, after that,' he said.

'Oh I will,' Liz assured him. 'Just take me across the pool first . . . Mm that's lovely.'

Kate turned away, unable to watch. She was remembering that last swimming lesson at Tarkawa Bay. Hastily she called out, 'I'm going back to do some work,' but neither of them heard her. She picked up her towel and went to her room to change.

Richard and Liz spent most of their off-duty time together during the next few days. Liz had developed a passion for swimming and Richard seemed keen to teach her. Kate was relieved when Sunday arrived and she could spend a whole day away from them. Mike had phoned to say that he would join her during the afternoon for a couple of hours, as he was on duty in the morning.

Chief Ladipo's car arrived promptly at ten o'clock. The driver, in a smart white suit with a chauffeur's cap, came briskly up the stairs to meet Kate, who was standing on the top of the steps. He removed his cap smartly, bowed very low and said, 'Madam, your car is ready.'

Kate went down the steps and got into the car. It was an enormous Cadillac with luxurious upholstery. She sank into the depths of the back seat and began to enjoy the feeling of unashamed luxury. The car purred its way down the drive, like some vast pampered feline. As they went through the village of Ikawa, the children playing outside their little houses waved as they saw the magnificent car speeding past.

Soon they arrived at Ladipo Palace. The driver leapt out and hurried to open the door for Kate. Then he led her up the wide stone steps to an impressive terrace. Marble pillars supported a mosaic roof, which shielded the terrace from the piercing rays of the sun.

The terrace led on to a magnificent courtyard with large stone vases full of flowers and plants; at the very centre, a huge fountain was playing. Kate had barely time to take it all in before Chief Ladipo appeared. His large body was draped in a colourful robe, which gave him the appearance of an ancient Roman king in a toga.

'Welcome, welcome my dear,' he beamed expansively as he came towards her and shook her hand vigorously. 'Where is your companion?'

'He's at the hospital. Can't get away until this afternoon.'

'Well, never mind; so much the better, I can have you all to myself,' he grinned mischievously. 'Come and meet my family.' He led her through a maze of cool corridors to the garden at the other side of the house. The gardens sloped down to a large oval-shaped swimming pool where the Ladipo family were enjoying themselves. Kate was introduced first to Mrs Ladipo, a handsome statuesque woman in a large floral swimsuit who smiled welcomingly.

'I am so glad you could come,' she said. 'My husband has told me so much about you. Come and meet the children.' She led Kate to the edge of the pool. There were six little black bodies swimming and splashing happily in the water. They came to the edge of the pool, reaching out their wet arms to shake hands with Kate. They smiled and laughed joyfully, displaying perfect white teeth.

'They're adorable,' said Kate when all the introductions had been made.

Chief Ladipo smiled proudly. 'I wanted you to meet my family,' he said. 'Would you like a swim, my dear?'

'I'm afraid, I haven't brought a swimsuit,' said Kate.

'No problem,' said Chief Ladipo. He clapped his hands and one of the stewards came forward. 'Take madam to the changing rooms,' he said, then turning to Kate he added, 'You'll find everything you need there.'

Kate followed the steward to a room at the edge of the garden. He opened the door and she went inside to find a large room which resembled the bathroom of a luxury hotel. A maid stepped forward and indicated the row of swimsuits and bikinis which were hanging in a long wardrobe. Kate chose an expensive-looking bikini which was her size, and changed quickly.

The children shouted gleefully as Kate jumped into the water. They crowded round her and swam beside her across the pool. Chief Ladipo joined them, looking like a friendly whale in his enormous blue swimsuit. He explained that his wife was not going to swim, as they were expecting their seventh happy event in a few months time.

The morning passed very quickly, until it was time for the children's nanny to take them away in preparation for lunch. Drinks were then served by the pool.

'Do you like Africa?' said Chief Ladipo as they sipped their drinks.

'I love it,' said Kate enthusiastically. 'I should like to stay here forever.'

'Then why don't you?' he said.

'I've got to go back to England soon,' she said quietly.

'But why?'

'There are problems at home. My fiancé . . .' she began.

'So you're engaged to be married,' he interrupted her.

'Yes,' Kate said.

'But that should be an occasion for rejoicing, my dear.'

'As I said, there are problems,' she continued.

'Yes, but if you love him, there are no problems,' he laughed. He reached out a large hand and patted his wife gently. 'My wife and I, we have no problems because we love each other. How do you say it in your country? "Love conquers all".'

Kate's eyes were moist with tears. Chief Ladipo looked concerned. He leaned towards her.

'My dear, if you don't love him you must not go back. Escape to freedom while you can. Your life is just as important as his.' He heaved his huge body out of the sun chair and looked round for the nearest steward. 'We will have lunch now,' he called.

'Yes, sir.' The steward hurried into the house.

After Kate had changed the maid showed her the way

to the dining room. It was a magnificent high-ceilinged room with windows leading to the garden on one side, and out to the courtyard, on the other. The six children, with two nannies in attendance, sat at one end of the table and Chief Ladipo sat at the head, between his wife and Kate. The children were extremely well-behaved and Kate marvelled at the table manners of even the tiniest child.

It was a sumptuous meal, comprising several courses. After the first three courses the nannies took the children away for their siesta. They had arrived at the coffee stage, and Chief Ladipo was lighting up a large cigar, when Mike was ushered in by a steward.

Chief Ladipo smiled in welcome and waved a large arm towards the vacant chair at Kate's side. 'Good to see you,' he said. 'Sit down, sit down. What can we get you? Have you had lunch?'

Mike sat down next to Kate. 'Yes thank you. I had lunch at the hospital. A coffee would be nice.'

'Of course,' Chief Ladipo beckoned to one of the stewards who came forward with a silver coffee pot. 'And a brandy, I think?' added the Chief.

'No, I don't think so,' said Mike. 'I've got to go back on duty in a couple of hours, so I'd better stay sober.'

Kate shook her head. 'Not for me, thank you; I'd better keep a clear head for this evening. I think I shall find there'll be a lot of work waiting for me when I get back.'

'Well enjoy yourselves while you can,' said Chief Ladipo, smiling as he sipped a large brandy. 'Come and see the gardens,' he said, when he had finished his brandy.

They wandered out along the paths between the flower beds.

'It's like a tropical paradise,' said Kate. 'I had no idea you could grow all these flowers in this soil.'

'I have my soil specially imported,' said the Chief. 'And I employ ten full-time gardeners. My wife loves flowers.' He smiled at his wife.

They sat by the side of the pool under a canopy which had been erected to shield them from the afternoon sun. Tea was served about four o'clock and then Mike said he would have to go back to the hospital. Turning to Kate he said,

'I'm glad you could make it today. I thought Richard might not let you out again for a while.'

'This Richard,' said Chief Ladipo, 'I presume you're talking about Dr Brooks?'

'That's right,' said Mike. 'I took Kate out the other night and we got back rather late. Richard was very annoyed.'

'You mean he was jealous,' said Chief Ladipo, laughing.

'Jealous?' said Mike. 'No, why should he be jealous?'

'Oh come now, I should have thought that was obvious. You take his pretty little nurse out for the evening, and you think he's not jealous.' Chief Ladipo laughed loudly. Mike was not amused.

'I must be going now,' he said as he stood up. He shook hands with the Chief and his wife. 'Thank you for your hospitality.'

'You must come again, when you can stay longer,' said Chief Ladipo. He called one of the stewards. 'Take Dr Gregson to his car.'

Kate stayed until the heat of the afternoon sun began to die down. She felt relaxed and refreshed after her day of luxury and was reluctantly casting her mind towards the prospect of going back on duty when one of the stewards came hurrying out of the house.

'A phone call for Madam,' he announced.

'For me?' said Kate. The steward was bringing a trolley with a phone on, to her side. 'Whoever can be phoning me here?'

It was Liz, in a great panic, 'Kate, I don't know what to do. Mr Brown has swallowed some tablets and he's out cold.'

'What tablets?' Kate's brain was immediately alert.

'I don't know. He broke open the poisons cupboard.'

'Give him a gastric lavage immediately,' said Kate. There was a pause, then Liz said,

'I don't know how to. Kate, what am I going to do?'

'I'll come at once,' said Kate quickly. She put the phone down and jumped to her feet. 'Emergency,' she said. 'I have to go.'

'My car is ready,' said Chief Ladipo. He hurried out to the front steps with her. The driver had already brought the car round.

'As quick as you can,' said Kate, to the driver. She turned briefly, 'Thank you for a marvellous day,' she had time to say before the Cadillac drove off at high speed. They made the journey in half the time it had taken in the morning.

Kate leapt out and dashed into the nursing home. She went straight to the patients' wing, and into Mr Brown's room. He lay motionless on the bed. There seemed to be no sign of life. Kate felt anxiously for his pulse and detected a weak throbbing. Quickly she administered a gastric lavage, watched helplessly by Liz who seemed unable to offer any assistance.

Several minutes passed before Mr Brown feebly opened his eyes. He looked at Kate in bewilderment. 'What happened?' he said.

'You tell me,' she said. 'You very nearly died just now. Another few minutes and it would have been too late.'

'Now I remember,' he muttered. 'I'm sorry, Nurse. I didn't mean to cause you all this trouble. I just felt so lonely, all by myself. Nobody had been to see me for hours.'

Kate glanced at Liz, who was still looking as if she was in a state of shock. 'Well, we'll talk about that later,' said Kate. 'Nurse Mason, do you think you could stay here for a few minutes.'

'Don't leave me, Nurse Mathews,' wailed Mr Brown, clinging to Kate's hand. 'Please don't leave me.'

Kate sat down at the side of the bed. 'No, I won't leave you just yet,' she said. 'Nurse Mason, did you ring Dr Brooks?'

'No, I didn't,' said Liz.

'Why ever not?' asked Kate.

Liz looked acutely embarrassed. 'I thought it would be better if you got back here first. I knew you would know what to do,' she said.

'Mm, I see. Well you'd better ring him now,' she said. Liz went off to the office. Kate stayed with Mr Brown for the remainder of the evening. He agreed to let her go when Joseph came on duty, and Kate instructed Joseph to watch him carefully and call her if there was any change. Thankfully she made her way to the office.

Liz had recovered some of her composure by now. 'Thanks, Kate,' she said. 'It was a good thing you came back when you did.'

'It certainly was a good thing,' said Kate severely. 'But you could have performed a gastric lavage by yourself, couldn't you?'

'I don't think so,' said Liz.

'But surely . . .' began Kate and then she stopped. An awful thought had crossed her mind. It was a suspicion which had been developing ever since she had started working with Liz. 'Where exactly did you train?' asked Kate quietly.

Liz looked frightened. 'What's that got to do with it?' she snapped. 'I don't think it's important.'

'Well I think it's important,' said Kate. 'Mr Brown very nearly died just now and I want to know why a so-called trained nurse didn't know how to handle the situation. I suppose that was why you wanted me to come back instead of Richard.'

Liz burst into tears. 'Oh Kate, please don't tell Richard,' she sobbed.

'Don't tell Richard what?' asked Kate.

'Don't tell him how I panicked,' said Liz quickly. 'I couldn't bear it.'

'Anyway, how did it happen that Mr Brown was able to get into the poisons cupboard?' asked Kate.

'I left the keys on the desk when I went for tea,' said Liz in a small voice. Her eyes looked appealingly at Kate. 'It won't happen again, I promise,' she said earnestly.

'You're dead right it won't,' said Kate. 'From now on I'm going to make sure you're never left in charge here.'

'But you won't tell Richard, will you?' she appealed.

'Liz, I've got to tell him something. He's the MD around here. A man attempts suicide while in his care; he's got to be told something. I would have thought he would have been back by now. When did you ring him?'

'I didn't,' said Liz quietly.

Kate was about to explode, when Richard walked through the door.

'Why were you going to ring me?' he asked.

Kate took a deep breath. 'There was a slight mishap here,' she said, pausing as she searched for the right words. 'Mr Brown took an overdose, but we've pumped him out and he'll live.'

'Good heavens!, it's a good thing you acted quickly,' he said. 'Well done girls. I'd no idea he was suicidal. I'll go and see him.'

'It's OK,' said Kate quickly. 'Joseph's with him. Don't disturb him at the moment; he's very tired.'

'All right, I'll go along later. Kate will you stay on tonight? I expect Liz is tired after her day on duty.' He smiled at Liz, who smiled back happily.

'Yes, I was going to stay on anyway,' said Kate. 'Joseph can cope with the other patients and I'll stay with Mr Brown.'

'Good girl,' said Richard. 'Come along, Liz, I expect you're ready for some dinner. Will you be coming over, Kate?'

'No thanks. I'll get Musa to bring me something on a tray. I'm not very hungry,' she said.

'I expect you've been living it up at Ladipo Palace,' said Richard. 'Some people have all the luck. Come on, Liz, let's go and see what's on the menu tonight.'

Kate sat down at the desk and waited until they had disappeared, then she picked up the phone and dialled the international code for France, followed by the number of the hotel on the Riviera, which her mother had given her.

'May I speak to Dr James Clark?' she said. After a short pause, the familiar voice said,

'Hello, James Clark here.'

'This is Kate.'

'Kate, darling, is there anything the matter?'

'No, no not really.' She tried to sound unconcerned.

'It's about Nurse Mason. Did you actually see her references and qualifications when you appointed her?'

'Well, no. The agency checked her out for me and I took their word. Why, what's the matter?'

'Oh nothing; it's just that I'd like to find out where she trained. Could you let me have the details?'

'Of course. Can it wait till we get back? I don't think I can contact the agency until then.'

'Certainly,' Kate tried to make her voice sound light. 'How's Mummy?'

'She's fine. We're having a marvellous time here, but I'm looking forward to going home to Scotland. You'll come and see us, won't you?'

'Of course. Give my love to Mummy. Goodbye.'

She felt a sense of relief, as she put the phone down. If what she suspected was true, then she would have to tell Richard, otherwise there was no point in alarming him. Meanwhile she would simply have to be extremely careful about the duties assigned to Liz.

CHAPTER TWELVE

THE next month was extremely difficult for Kate. She insisted on supervising everything Liz did in the patients' wing, and found it something of a strain. Richard called her into the office one day and challenged her about it.

'Kate, don't you think you're being over-zealous in the way you watch over Liz? Perhaps if you gave her less supervision she might develop a sense of responsibility.'

Kate paused before answering. It would be such a comfort to share her suspicion with Richard, but it was, after all, only a suspicion. She must not shatter his illusions about Liz. If only Dr Clark would contact her, she would know how to act.

'Richard, I'm sorry if you disapprove of my nursing methods, but I think Liz needs a lot of help. This is her first time in the tropics, after all.'

'Well, I suppose you know what you're doing,' he said grudgingly. 'But you do seem to be wearing yourself out. You've been looking very tired recently. Would you like to come out to Tarkawa Bay on Sunday?'

Kate looked startled. 'I don't think we should leave Liz in charge,' she said quickly.

'I wasn't thinking of leaving Liz,' he said. 'John told me to bring a party. He said he would arrange for someone to cover the nursing home, if necessary—probably Sister Jones. She's reliable enough, don't you think?'

'Yes, of course. I'd love to come, if you can make the necessary arrangements.'

'Good, that's settled then,' he smiled at her. 'The sea air will do you good.'

'Who's going?' Kate asked.

'Well Liz, of course . . .' he started.

'Of course . . .' repeated Kate quietly.

'And John and Helen and the children,' he continued.

'How about Mike?' said Kate quickly. 'Is he invited?'

'I'm sure John would include him if you like,' said Richard evenly. 'I'll give him a ring.'

'Yes, do that,' said Kate. She had no intention of playing gooseberry to the two love birds.

Everyone met down by the harbour on Sunday morning. Kate had arranged for Musa to pack a hamper of food and Helen also had a large box.

'We look as if we're going to stay for a week,' laughed John, as they loaded the boat.

'We shall all be starving, when we've had a swim,' said Richard.

John steered the boat round the coast and headed for Tarkawa Bay. They sailed smoothly through the blue water, which was unruffled by the slightest breeze. The hot sun beat mercilessly down upon them. As soon as they reached the beach hut, everybody stripped off and rushed into the sea to cool down. John and Helen stayed in the shallow water with the children, but Richard and Mike headed out to sea.

'Come on, girls,' Richard called. 'It's much better out here.' Kate started to swim out, but Liz remained behind.

'Richard, I daren't go out of my depth,' she wailed. 'You know I can't swim very well. Come and help me.' She held out her arms imploringly.

Richard obediently returned towards the shore and started to carry Liz along with him. She lay on her back and allowed herself to be taken out to the calm waters beyond the breakers. Mike swam along by the side of Kate, until the four of them were together.

'Isn't it beautiful out here,' said Liz. 'I didn't think I would ever have the nerve to swim out this far.'

Richard laughed. 'I wasn't aware that you had actually done any swimming yet,' he said. 'Why don't you try now.' He released his hold on her and she started to sink.

'Richard!' she screamed. 'Help me!' Her arms flailing in all directions, she grabbed Richard round the neck and clung tightly.

'OK, OK,' he said. 'You haven't learned as quickly as my last pupil,' he added, smiling at Kate.

'Come on, I think this is far enough for the girls,' said Mike. 'Race you back to the shore, Kate.' They set off through the calm water, plunged through the breakers and found themselves carried rapidly on to the shore. Kate was several yards behind Mike but he waited for her and scooped her up in his arms.

'A dead heat,' he laughed. 'Well done Kate.' Then he tossed her back into the water.

'You beast,' she cried, as she struggled out of the sea and chased him along the sand. They both fell laughing and exhausted into a sandy hollow at the edge of the beach.

'Richard seems to be giving Liz a long swimming lesson,' said Mike as they looked out to sea.

'Mm, Liz seems to enjoy her swimming lessons,' said Kate.

'I don't think it's the swimming she enjoys,' said Mike. 'She's obviously decided that Richard is a good catch, and he seems to have fallen for it. How's your lover-boy back home, by the way?'

'He's fine,' said Kate lightly.

'It's still on then?'

'Of course.'

'Funny; you never talk about him.'

'Why should I?'

'No reason. I thought maybe you were cooling off.'

'No, I'm going back next month.'

'I shall miss you, Kate,' he said.

'I shall miss you, Mike. You've been a good friend.'

'So you keep telling me,' he grinned wryly.

'Come on, let's go and help with the barbecue,' said Kate briskly. They ran along the beach back to where John was lighting the fire.

'Need any help, John?' called Mike.

'Most certainly do. Can you gather some more driftwood?'

'Sure. Come and help me, kids.' The children ran happily towards Mike.

'I'll go and help Helen,' said Kate, as she went towards the beach-hut. She found Helen unpacking the food. 'Here, let me give you a hand,' she said.

'Thanks,' said Helen. 'I thought I'd prepare the chickens in here and then carry them out. Will you deal with the salad, Kate?'

The two women worked side by side until the food was ready to be taken outside. Helen poured out two glasses of fruit juice and handed one to Kate.

'It's thirsty work,' she said. 'I thought Richard and Liz would have been back by now.'

'They're having a long swimming lesson, I think,' said Kate.

'Mm. Strange how Richard seems to have taken to

Liz,' said Helen quietly. 'I mean she's not his type at all. Still, I suppose he decided to settle for second best under the circumstances.'

'What circumstances?' said Kate evenly.

Helen smiled, 'Come on; don't pretend, Kate.' She picked up a tray of food. 'Let's join the others.'

Kate followed Helen out to the barbecue. John had succeeded in lighting a good fire which was beginning to settle down to the right temperature. Mike and the children were still combing the beach and had built a huge pile of wood.

'That's enough,' shouted John. 'We're only here for a day.' He smiled as Kate and Helen arrived. 'I think we could survive here for a week at least,' he said. 'We've got enough food and wood.'

'Great,' laughed Helen. 'Let's cancel all engagements and stay here.'

'There's no phone,' he said, in mock concern.

'Pity—we can't cancel engagements if we've no phone,' agreed Helen. 'OK, let's enjoy what we've got.'

'Shall I start cooking?' said John. 'Where on earth have those two got to? Oh, here they are.'

Liz and Richard were walking hand in hand out of the sea.

'Just in time,' called John. 'Will you pour the drinks, Mike. I'll put the chickens on.'

'I shall have to change my bikini,' said Liz as she arrived at the fire.

'Whatever for?' asked Helen. 'It will dry in seconds, in this heat.'

'I think the salt-water will spoil it,' said Liz. 'Is there somewhere I can rinse it out?'

'Oh yes. Every mod. con. out here on the tropical isle,' said Kate gaily. 'Come on, I'll show you.'

Liz followed Kate into the hut. 'It's all so primitive in here,' she said.

'What did you expect?' asked Kate. 'That's the fun of the place. You can change over there and there's a bowl here to rinse out your bikini, but for heavens' sake don't take all the fresh water.'

'Do you think you could do it for me?' said Liz, in her quiet little-girl voice.

'No, I most certainly could not,' said Kate firmly and went back to the barbecue, leaving Liz to cope as best she could.

Everyone was sitting round the fire watching the sizzling chickens. Richard handed her a drink. 'Did you have a good swim?' he asked.

'Mm. Did you?'

'Not much swimming. More life-saving than anything else,' he laughed. 'Liz seems like a slow-learner.'

'She'll need lots of lessons, then,' said Mike.

'I expect so,' Richard said.

John had already served the chicken when Liz emerged from the beach-hut, wearing a long red skirt and a matching sun top. She had brushed out her blonde hair so that it fell smoothly down her back, glinting in the sunlight.

'The goddess approaches,' grinned Mike.

'Ssh,' said Helen. 'She'll hear you. She's certainly made an effort. I feel quite grubby.'

'Oh, she's made an effort all right,' said Mike dryly.

Richard had already gone to meet Liz. Mike stood up gallantly and offered her his chair, which she accepted.

When everyone had finished lunch, they lay around in the shade of the trees. Kate and Helen cleared away the remains of the food, to prevent the flies and ants from gathering. Liz removed her long skirt and sun top to reveal a matching bikini, and smoothed sun-tan oil over her long slim legs.

'Richard,' she called plaintively, 'I can't reach my back. Be a darling and rub this stuff on for me.'

Looking slightly embarrassed, Richard complied, then sat down next to Mike who was watching the dying embers.

'John, have you still got your snorkel and goggles out here?' Mike asked suddenly.

'Yes, do you want to borrow them?'

'Yes, I'd like to swim out and have a look at some of the tropical fish beyond the breakers.'

'OK, I'll get them for you.' John went towards the hut.

'Can I come with you?' said Liz, rolling over lazily, to look at Mike.

'I can't cope with you and look at the fish,' said Mike. 'Why don't you stay here and have a rest?'

'There's a lilo in the hut. I could lie on that and rest on the water,' she said. 'May I borrow it, Helen?'

'Of course, if Mike thinks it's a good idea,' said Helen.

'You'd better make sure you stay on it,' said Mike firmly. 'I can't life-save you if I've got my head under water.'

Mike set off down the beach carrying the snorkel, goggles and lilo with Liz following behind. Helen and John took the children into the hut for a siesta. Kate closed her eyes and found herself falling asleep in the afternoon heat. She was drifting off into a dream world when suddenly there was a loud cry from the water.

'Mike!' Liz was screaming. 'Mike, save me!'

Kate and Richard were on their feet at once, 'My god, she's fallen off,' said Kate. 'Why doesn't Mike do something?'

'He can't hear her,' said Richard. 'He's got the goggles and snorkel on and his head is under water.

'Richard, she'll drown out there.' Kate was sprinting towards the sea but Richard overtook her. He plunged into the waves and made towards the upturned lilo, which was already drifting out to sea. Liz's head appeared above the water for a brief second, then submerged again. Richard swam quickly through the breakers towards her. She came to the surface again and Richard took hold of her, firmly pulling her along, back to the shore.

At that moment, Mike lifted his head out of the water and saw the empty lilo. He looked round anxiously until he saw Richard pulling Liz through the waves. Quickly he plunged back through the breakers and swam to the beach. Richard had already carried Liz to the fire-side and put her down on a bed of towels, where she lay with her eyes closed.

'I'm sorry,' said Mike as he rushed up the beach. 'What happened?'

'It's not your fault,' said Richard. 'I can't see how she came to fall off. The water was calm enough.'

'Oh, Richard, don't be cross with me,' said Liz, opening her eyes and looking at him helplessly. 'I couldn't help it. You should have been out there with me, then it wouldn't have happened. But I'm so glad you saved me. Thank you, darling.' She continued to play the helpless victim for the rest of the afternoon, enjoying the extra fuss and attention.

The Millers were alarmed when they came out of the hut after their siesta and saw Liz stretched out on the towels.

'It's a good thing you're a strong swimmer, Richard,' said John.

'Sorry about the lilo,' said Mike.

'It doesn't matter,' said Helen. 'The main thing is that Liz was saved. How did you come to fall off, my dear?' she asked Liz, quietly.

'I really don't know,' said Liz. 'I think I must have fallen asleep.'

Mike jumped up, 'Come on, Kate, let's go for a walk.' When they were out of earshot he turned to her and said, 'I think Liz staged the whole thing just to get Richard to lifesave her.'

'Don't be silly,' said Kate. 'Why would she want to do that?'

'I've told you, she's desperate to get Richard,' said Mike. 'There's something phoney about that girl, don't you think?'

'There could be,' Kate said quietly. 'I'm not sure.'

'So you do think so?' said Mike.

Kate paused. 'I don't want to alarm Richard, but I don't think she's got any qualifications. I rang Dr Clark to get him to check with the agency, but that was a month ago and so far I've heard nothing.'

'You poor girl,' said Mike. 'But why haven't you told Richard?'

'I think he's in love with her,' Kate said quietly. 'There's no point in shattering his illusions unless I have to.'

'Well let me know how things develop, and if there's anything I can do to help, you've only got to ask.'

'Thanks Mike . . .' she started.

'Don't say it,' he interrupted, smiling. 'I'm a good friend.'

They both laughed.

They walked along the beach as far as the rocks where Kate and Richard had rested on their last visit to Tarkawa. The sun was beginning to get lower in the sky.

'Let's go back now,' said Kate. 'This place gives me the shivers.'

'In this heat?' he laughed. 'What a funny girl you are.'

They made their way back to the beach-hut, where Helen, John and Richard were beginning to pack the things into the boat.

'It's been a marvellous day,' Kate said when they were all safely on board. 'I do love Tarkawa.'

'Well you must be sure to come out with us again before you go back,' said Helen. 'How much longer do you have out here?'

'Three weeks,' said Kate.

'Is that all?' said John. 'You must certainly come over to dinner before you leave us.' He steered the boat steadily round the coast, back to Kyruba harbour.

Liz was still feeling fragile after her ordeal and had to be helped into the car. She lay across the back seat, propped up on cushions, and Kate sat in the front with Richard. When they arrived at Ikawa, Richard said,

'Kate, will you help Liz into bed, while I go and take a report from Margaret Jones. Perhaps you could ask Musa to take her supper on a tray.'

'Oh, I'm really not very hungry,' said Liz weakly. 'Kate could scramble me some eggs or something.'

'Kate is not employed as a cook here,' said Richard evenly. 'I'm sure Musa will bring you something from the kitchen. Kate, when you've changed I'd like you to help me.'

'Of course,' said Kate. She helped Liz to her room, called for Musa and then changed into her uniform. She found herself looking forward to a spell on duty, without Liz. Recently she had found the work stimulating. Many of the medical problems had been sorted out. Mrs Marshall had been transferred to a private room at Kyruba hospital where she could have a daily consultation with the psychiatrist. Mr Brown had responded well to the new drug therapy and had been able to go home. Kate found that her main problem on duty was coping with Liz. Now that she was safely tucked up in bed, it would be possible to run the patients' wing with the minimum of effort. She decided that if there was no reply from Dr Clark soon, she would contact him again.

To her delight there were two letters by her plate next morning at breakfast. Hurriedly she opened the one on which she recognised Dr Clark's handwriting. It had come from Scotland.

'My dear Kate,' he wrote 'I called into the agency on our way through London and gave them your request. They said it might take some time, as they will have to contact referees etc, so you might not hear from them for a few weeks. I do hope this isn't urgent. Please let me know if you are having problems.

'Your mother sends her love. We have had a splendid honeymoon and are now enjoying the beautiful countryside of Scotland . . .' The letter went on to describe what was happening on the estate but Kate's eyes remained riveted to the words '. . . you might not hear from them for a few weeks'.

'Not bad news, I hope,' said Richard.

'No, oh no . . . I was miles away,' she said quickly. 'Dr Clark sends his regards to you.'

'I suppose your other letter is from the faithful fiancé,' he said.

'Yes it is,' said Kate, tearing it open. It was full of news of the practice and the new nurse who was helping them.

At the end David had devoted a whole paragraph to telling her how he was longing to have her back with him. She looked up from the letter and saw that Richard was watching her closely.

'So you're really going through with it,' he said.

She swallowed hard. Yes, of course.'

'There were times when I didn't think you would,' he said quietly, almost to himself. Briskly he stood up. 'How's Liz today?' he asked.

'She's a little tired, so I've told her to stay in bed,' said Kate.

'Can you cope by yourself?'

'Of course.'

'Fine. I've got to go down to Kyruba. It's my final interview for the medical consultancy today.'

'Good luck, Richard.'

'Thanks. I'll need it.'

'I hope you get the job.'

'Do you? It won't make any difference to you, tucked away in your neat little English village.' He strode purposefully across the verandah and out to his car.

Kate made her way to the patients' wing and threw herself into her work. Richard returned during the afternoon and came on duty looking slightly despondent.

'Well, how did it go?' asked Kate.

'I don't really know. It could go either way. I shan't hear for a couple of weeks at least. They're still interviewing the other candidates. How are things here?'

'Fine; no problems.'

'You're still alone, I see,' said Richard.

'Yes, I told Liz I could manage. She says she still feels weak.'

'Strange, how it happened yesterday,' said Richard.

'Mm, very strange.'

'You do seem to be doing all the work around here,' said Richard. 'I shall be glad when Julie gets back from leave. When is it exactly?'

'In two weeks. We shall have a few days together before I go,' said Kate.

'I expect Liz will be fit to take over from you by then,' he said.

'I hope so,' said Kate firmly. 'I certainly hope so.'

Richard was intrigued by her tone of voice. 'Kate are you keeping something from me?' he asked. 'I know you don't like Liz, but is there any special reason for it?'

'You mean, apart from the fact that I have to do all her work as well as my own,' she answered lightly.

'Only because you choose to,' he snapped. 'If you allowed her to do more, she might learn something. Instead you insist on playing the big martyr. Florence Nightingale doing it alone!'

'Richard, I don't want to discuss it. Let's leave it shall we.'

'I suppose you're practising for your good-little-wife role,' he continued relentlessly. 'Throwing yourself away on the first man you meet . . .'

'That's enough!' she cried. 'I have my reasons for disliking Liz; I have my reasons for marrying David. Now leave me alone.'

'I'll leave you alone,' he said in a cold voice. 'I'm going to get Liz back on duty. I think you need a break.'

'Yes. I do need a break. You're quite right,' she said. 'I shall go to England the minute Julie returns.'

Angrily she flicked through the official diary on the desk. 'Here it is Richard,' she said. 'October 15th, Julie back from leave. Fine, I'll book myself on the evening plane. Will that suit you?'

'Perfectly,' he said coldly. 'I'll go and find Liz.' He stood up and made his way across the garden to her room.

Kate picked up the phone and rang the airport.

CHAPTER THIRTEEN

HAVING decided to return as soon as possible, Kate found that her time was fully occupied with preparations. She had reluctantly to turn down an invitation to spend Sunday at Tarkawa again.

'I'm sorry, Helen,' she said on the phone. 'I've just got too much to do before I go home.'

'Well, come over for dinner one evening then,' said Helen.

'Yes, I'd love to. I'll arrange it with Richard.'

'Richard must come too.'

'No, he'll have to stay with Liz,' said Kate quickly.

There was a pause, then Helen asked, 'Shall I invite Mike?'

'Yes, that would be nice,' said Kate.

Richard coolly agreed that Kate should be off-duty for the evening of the dinner. He seemed perfectly happy to stay behind with Liz.

Helen had prepared a delightful meal for the four of them. Afterwards they sat on the verandah in the moonlight, drinking coffee and gazing at the millions of stars clustered above them.

'I can't believe I shall really be in England next week, looking at these same stars,' said Kate.

'Don't talk about it,' said Mike. 'I'm going to miss you terribly.'

'We all are,' said Helen.

'I'm going to miss you too,' said Kate. 'And I'm going to hate saying goodbye to this darling old house for the last time. It's like parting with a piece of my life.' She tried to smile but the tears were not far away.

'Did you know Richard has made me an offer for this place?' said John.

'No, I didn't,' said Kate in surprise, 'I didn't know you had decided to sell it yet.'

'We've got to sell it, so we can buy the nursing home,' said Helen. 'We can't afford both.'

'Why does Richard want to buy it?' asked Kate.

'I'm not sure. He was very mysterious,' said John. 'He said something about a man having to settle down some time. He's not thinking of getting married again, is he?'

'Not as far as I know,' said Mike. 'Still, you never know with Richard, do you, Kate?'

'No, he's a dark horse,' she said quietly.

'Certainly is,' agreed Mike.

Later, as he drove her home he returned to the subject of Richard. 'You know, he never ceases to amaze me,' he said. 'I mean, when he started taking Liz around, I thought he was just having a bit of fun. But it seems to be serious, doesn't it? Do you think he's really planning to marry her?'

'I honestly couldn't say,' said Kate.

'Well, there's no doubt what her answer will be, if and when he pops the question,' continued Mike. 'I say, have you heard anything from Dr Clark about Liz's background?'

'Only that the agency is checking up and it may take some time.'

'Don't you think you ought to say something to Richard?' asked Mike.

'No, he'd only think I was imagining things. He already thinks I've got my knife into her.'

'Well, I hope you hear soon.'

'So do I,' said Kate emphatically.

Mike pulled up outside the nursing home and opened the car door. They went up the steps together. On the top step, Mike paused. 'I won't invite myself in again,' he said, with a wry grin. 'I remember what happened last time.'

Kate smiled. 'Let me say it, Mike. You've been a good friend.'

He smiled and tried to make a joke. 'A friend in need . . .' he started and then stopped. Leaning forward he kissed her lightly on the cheek. 'Goodbye Kate,' he said, and went quickly back to his car.

Kate stood on the steps and waved as he drove off in the moonlight. Then she turned away and went into the house. She noticed a light in Richard's office as she passed. His door was half open so she put her head round. Richard was sitting at his desk, sorting through some papers. He looked up and smiled wearily.

'You're working late,' said Kate. 'What's the panic?'

'No panic. Just trying to sort things out for the new boss.'

'You mean John Miller? When does he take over?' asked Kate.

'As soon as the solicitors have tied all the legal knots.'

'And what about his house?' asked Kate as innocently as possible.

'What about his house?' he repeated evenly.

'A little bird told me . . .' she started.

'Ah . . . news travels fast around here. I suppose John told you about my offer?'

'He just mentioned it in passing,' she said lightly. 'Will you live there all by yourself?'

'I might, and then again, I might not,' he said cryptically. 'I don't think you need to worry about me, Kate,' he added coldly.

'I'm not worrying about you,' she said. 'I have the utmost confidence in your judgment. But . . .' she paused. Richard was watching her with concern.

'Well come on, don't stop there,' he said. 'What are you trying to tell me?'

She took a deep breath. 'Oh, nothing.' He had made his bed; let him lie on it. 'Goodnight, Richard.'

'Goodnight, Kate.'

Richard had already returned to his paperwork. Kate walked across the garden to her room. The beauty of the tropical night never ceased to delight her. She loved the droning of the insects, the fragrance of the frangipani.

'I'm going to miss all this,' she thought. 'I'm going to miss so much when I leave Africa.'

Next morning there was a phone call from Chief Ladipo, exhorting Kate to spend an afternoon with his family, before she left for England. She said she would try to fit it in with her busy schedule as she wanted to say goodbye to the Ladipos. Richard gave her an afternoon off duty during the course of the week and she spent a couple of happy hours at Ladipo Palace. There were tearful goodbyes on both sides when Kate had to leave the Ladipo family. The children clung to her and begged her to return soon. Kate said she had no idea when it would be but she intended to return one day.

The evening before she was due to go back to England Musa had prepared a special dinner. He proudly served Kate, Richard and Liz in the dining room and basked in the praise which was lavished upon him.

'This is splendid,' said Richard. 'A positive banquet.'

'I think we should have a celebration dinner every night,' said Liz.

'This is not a celebration, Liz,' said Richard quickly. 'We are saying goodbye to Kate. Hardly a cause for celebration.' He smiled at Kate and raised his glass. 'Thank you for all your hard work.'

Kate smiled back at him. 'I've enjoyed my time here—well most of it,' she laughed uneasily.

'I thought you were going to make a farewell speech,' said Liz. 'I think you should, you know.'

A lump came into Kate's throat. 'There's really nothing more I can say.' Her voice trembled. 'Except . . . I hope everything works out OK here.'

'I don't see why it shouldn't,' said Liz firmly. She raised her glass and touched Richard's. 'Here's to the new medical consultant of Kyruba hospital.'

'Hey, steady on,' he said. 'Don't let's count our chickens before they're hatched.'

'Oh, you'll get it, I'm sure,' she said. 'And I shall be so proud of you,' she added possessively.

'When do you hear about it?' asked Kate quickly.

'They want to see me at the hospital tomorrow,' said Richard. 'That could be good or it could be bad. I'll just have to wait and see.'

'What an interesting day it will be tomorrow,' said Liz. 'Julie comes back, Kate leaves us, Richard hears the news. I can hardly wait.'

Kate excused herself from the dinner table as soon as she possibly could and made for the privacy of her little room. She finished her packing, took a shower and went to bed early.

The next morning she had an early breakfast so that she could finish off her work on the patients' wing. She wanted to write a detailed report for Julie to consult on her return that afternoon. It was quiet in the office and Kate had almost finished writing when the phone rang.

She picked it up immediately. A man's voice asked to speak to Nurse Liz Mason.

'Who's calling?' asked Kate automatically.

There was a pause and then the voice said, 'This is her father speaking.'

'Just a moment, Mr Mason. I'll see if I can find her for you.' Kate picked up the internal phone and dialled Liz's room. There was no reply, so she tried the dining room. Musa answered and said that Nurse Mason was on her way over to the patients' wing. Kate went out into the corridor to look for her, just as she came round the corner.

'There's a phone call for you, Liz. It's your father,' said Kate.

Liz seemed surprised. Kate went back to her report, and Liz picked up the phone.

'Hello, Daddy,' she began and then listened for a full two minutes before speaking again. Kate was trying to concentrate on her report, but she became aware that Liz was becoming more and more anxious as she listened to her father. Finally Liz said, 'Look, I can't talk here, I'll phone you later.' There was a short pause then Liz snapped, 'Yes, of course I will. I'm not stupid you know. OK . . . yes. I get the message, goodbye.' Angrily she slammed the phone down, then, remembering Kate, she tried to regain her composure.

Kate looked up from her report. 'Trouble?' she asked quietly.

'No, nothing I can't handle,' said Liz coolly. 'I've got to make a phone call. Could you finish that report later, Kate?'

Kate stood up. 'Of course, carry on. I'll go and start the morning routine. Perhaps you'll join me when you've finished,' she added as she left the office.

It was mid-morning before Liz came to help Kate, by which time most of the work was finished. Kate looked at her closely when she arrived. She seemed agitated and nervous.

'Come and have a coffee,' said Kate, 'You look as if you need one.'

'I'm all right,' said Liz quickly, but she seemed grateful for the coffee which Kate poured for her in the office.

'Everything under control?' asked Kate.

'Mm.' Liz was thoughtful as she sipped her coffee. There was silence for a short time, then Liz looked anxiously at Kate and said, 'What time does Julie get back today?'

'Four o'clock at the airport. Why?'

'I thought I might go and meet her,' said Liz unexpectedly.

'Go and meet her?' repeated Kate in surprise. 'I wasn't aware that you had any burning desire to renew her acquaintance,' she added tartly.

'I'd just like to get out for a while,' said Liz quickly. 'Besides, it's better if you're left in charge here.'

'I suppose so,' said Kate. 'Although I would have liked to meet her myself. You'd better bring her straight back, because there's only a short time for me to give her my report before I go. I'll go and tell Buba.'

'I don't need a driver,' said Liz quickly.

'I think you do,' Kate said firmly, as she went off to find Buba.

After lunch, Liz went to her room to get ready for the trip to the airport. Kate went back to the office to put the finishing touches to her report. She was pleased with what she had accomplished in her six months at the nursing home and a feeling of deep satisfaction crept over her. At the same time she could not ignore the sadness she experienced whenever she thought about leaving. She put down her pen and looked up to find Richard standing in the doorway, watching her.

'I'm just off to Kyruba,' he said gruffly. 'Everything under control here?'

'Of course,' answered Kate. 'I've finished my report for Julie.'

'Good . . .' he paused and cleared his throat nervously. 'Are you going to meet her?'

'No, Liz said she wanted to go,' said Kate.

'Good heavens!' Richard smiled. 'Perhaps she's going to make her peace with Julie. I hope so.'

'So do I,' said Kate quietly.

'What time do you leave?' asked Richard.

'About six.'

'I may not be back by then.'

'Then we must say goodbye,' said Kate lightly. She stood up and held out her hand across the desk. Richard came forward and took it firmly in his own. Their eyes met but neither of them showed any emotion. Richard leaned forward and kissed Kate lightly on the cheek.

'Goodbye,' he whispered, and turning hurriedly, he left the room.

Kate stood quite still, listening to the loud beating of her heart. Then she took a deep breath and walked across the office and out into the corridor. This was her last afternoon on duty at Ikawa Nursing Home. She was going to keep herself very busy so that she had no time to think.

Some time later she heard Buba and Liz drive off to the airport to fetch Julie. The hot afternoon wore on; there was very little to do as most of the patients were asleep. Kate found herself wishing that Julie would arrive so that she could hand over her responsibility and start living her own life again. She wanted to forget Ikawa, Kyruba, Matala; Africa and start again with David. Everything would work out when she got back to England. Joseph came to relieve her at four o'clock so she went over to her room to finish packing. Then she went on to the verandah to wait for Julie.

There was the sound of tyres on the gravel drive and Buba drove up to the front steps. Kate went out to meet the car. Julie jumped out of the back seat and came running towards her. They hugged each other like long-lost friends.

'Welcome back, Julie. You're looking well,' said Kate.

'I'm feeling well. I've had a marvellous holiday,' said Julie happily.

They started to go up the steps, but Kate turned and looked back at the car.

'Where's Liz?' she asked.

'Liz?' asked Julie. 'I don't know. Where should she be?'

'She came to meet you, in the car.'

'To meet me?' repeated Julie incredulously. 'Well I never saw her. Buba, what happened to Nurse Mason?'

Buba was carrying luggage up the steps; he stopped and put the cases down. 'She came to airport with me. She tell me she thirsty—she go for drink. She say come back, pick me up tonight when I go take Nurse Mathews.'

'How very odd,' said Kate. 'I thought she was up to something when she said she wanted to meet you. She's been acting strangely all day.'

'I'd forgotten about Liz,' said Julie. 'Has she improved at all?'

'Not a bit,' said Kate. 'In fact . . .' she waited until

Buba had gone into the house, then continued. 'I'm rather worried. I have a sneaking suspicion that we may have been deceived. I'm waiting to hear from the agency who employed her. As soon as they've checked her credentials, they're going to let me know.'

'Good girl. I'm glad you thought of that. What does Richard think?' asked Julie.

'I haven't told him anything about it,' said Kate.

Julie's eyes widened. 'But why ever not?' she asked.

'Because, I don't think he'd believe me. He's besotted by her—I think he's asked her to marry him,' she added quietly.

'No,' said Julie in amazement. 'I don't believe it.'

'So, under the circumstances, I thought it best to keep my suspicions to myself. We should be hearing from the agency soon. I'm afraid you'll have to handle it, Julie.'

'It will be a pleasure,' said Julie grimly. 'Come on let's go and get some tea and then you can give me your report. We haven't got much time before you go.'

The time passed quickly and at six o'clock Kate found herself standing outside with Julie, waiting for Buba to bring the car round.

'I'm going to miss you, Kate,' said Julie sadly. 'We must keep in touch.'

'I'll write when I get back to England,' said Kate.

Buba carried her cases to the car. She climbed in and they were off down the drive. Julie stood on the steps waving until they were out of sight.

Buba drove the car rapidly along the dusty road. Kate found herself wondering what explanation Liz would give for having stayed away all the afternoon. She closed her eyes and leaned back against the seat. Suddenly there was a screech of tyres and Kate opened her eyes. They had gone round a bend to find a car speeding towards them on the wrong side of the road. A head-on collision seemed inevitable, but at the last moment Buba swerved to avoid the car. Kate caught a glimpse of a blonde woman at the wheel, gazing ahead with a wide-eyed stare, before she saw the car veer off the road and crash into a tree. Buba pulled up at the side of the road, and he and Kate ran over to the crashed car.

The woman driver was slumped over the wheel. Kate undid her seat-belt and gave her a brief examination. The impact had been softened by the heavy under-growth around the tree and the woman seemed unhurt. Nevertheless, she was moaning and rolling her eyes in a bewildered fashion. Kate recognised immediately that there was some medical reason for her irrational be-haviour. At the same time she was concerned to find two small girls crying unhappily on the back seat.

'Mummy's poorly,' cried the bigger child who looked about five years old. 'Daddy said she had to see a doctor.'

Kate climbed into the back seat beside the children. 'Where is your daddy?' she asked gently.

'He's gone on a plane,' said the five year old. 'We took him to the plane and then Mummy said she had to see the doctor. She gets poorly sometimes.'

Kate turned her attention to the mother who seemed to be lapsing into a coma. After a brief examination, she turned to Buba and said, 'We must take her to the nursing home as quickly as possible. I can't be sure until we've made a thorough examination, but I think she needs insulin. Help me get her into our car.'

It was several minutes before they were able to drive off, with the mother and her two children safely in the car. Kate managed to establish the names of the children. They were Fiona who was five and Alison who was three. Fiona had sustained a deep cut down the side of her leg which Kate had to bind up. She made a mental note that it would require stitching as soon as possible.

Buba drove quickly back to the nursing home. As he turned into the drive Kate saw that Richard had just arrived and was climbing out of his car. She called to him.

'Richard, come and help me. We've got an emergency.'

Richard opened the car door and helped Kate to get out.

'What happened?' he asked.

'Car crash,' she said briefly. 'This child will need sutures in the leg. The mother is in a coma. You'd better examine her—I think she may be diabetic.'

Buba had already brought a stretcher and was helping Richard to put the mother on it. The children whimpered uneasily and Kate tried to comfort them. Julie came out on to the steps on hearing the noise and came to the car to help Kate. Together they took the children to the patients' wing. They examined them briefly to check for injuries and found that apart from Fiona's leg wound and a few bruises they were unharmed.

Kate stitched Fiona's leg, assuring her that it would be as good as new when it healed. When Kate had finished, Fiona clung to her, crying miserably.

'Don't leave me please. I'm frightened.'

'There's nothing to be frightened of. You're safe now,' said Kate soothingly. 'We'll find you a nice bed and you can stay with us until mummy's feeling better.'

Julie went off to help Richard with the mother, and Kate got both the children ready for bed. She put them into a twin-bedded room and then sat down between the beds. They both clung to her with their tiny hands.

She started to tell them a story about fairies and elves and pixies, making it up as she went along. Gradually their eyes started to close and they fell asleep. Kate tucked them in; she still did not dare to leave them, in case they woke up, so she sat quietly in the room listening to the steady rhythm of their breathing. It was only then that she remembered she had missed her plane. There had been no time to think about herself. She also remembered Liz and wondered if she was still waiting at the airport.

'I expect she's got a taxi back here by now,' she thought, as she closed her eyes wearily. The next thing she knew Julie was standing beside her, with a hand on her shoulder.

'I'm sorry to waken you, Kate,' she said. 'But what do you think we should do about Liz?'

'Hasn't she come back yet?' said Kate, rubbing her hands across her eyes in an effort to wake up.

'No, I've only just thought about her,' said Julie.

'What time is it?' asked Kate anxiously.

'It's after midnight,' said Julie.

'What?' Kate sat bolt upright in her chair. 'I'm glad you woke me. Where's Richard?'

'He's looking after the diabetic mother. I think we've got her stabilised at last.'

'We'd better not worry him about Liz,' said Kate. 'Let's ring the airport and see if she's still there.'

'I'll do it,' said Julie. 'You'd better stay with the children.'

She went to the office. Several minutes later she came back to say that the airport staff were looking for Liz and would ring if they had anything to report. 'Don't say anything to Richard until we hear from them,' said Julie.

'He's desperately tired and I think he thinks Liz is safely tucked up in bed.'

'Have you heard if he's got the job of medical consultant?' asked Kate.

'We were so busy, I didn't have time to ask him,' said Julie. 'I'll ask him tomorrow. Do you want me to relieve you here for a while?'

'No, that's OK,' said Kate. 'The children are used to me. I'd better stay until they wake up.'

'Well, make yourself comfortable,' said Julie. 'Joseph's out there at the desk if you need anything.'

'Thanks, I shall be all right. Goodnight, Julie.'

'Goodnight, Kate.'

Kate looked at the sleeping children, then closed her eyes and went back to sleep.

CHAPTER FOURTEEN

KATE woke early next morning. At first she could not think where she was, as she stirred in the big armchair. Then she remembered the events of the previous night. The children were sleeping peacefully in their beds so she got up and went along the corridor. Richard was sitting at the desk. He looked up wearily as she approached.

'Have you been here all night?' he asked.

'Yes, I didn't want to leave the children. How's their mother?'

'She's comfortable now. The children will be able to see her when they wake. Your diagnosis was correct, Nurse,' he added, smiling at her.

She smiled back. 'Glad to be of service, Doctor,' she grinned.

'You'd better take a few hours off,' said Richard. 'I'll get Liz to come and take over from you.' He reached for the phone. Quickly Kate stopped him.

'Richard, there's something you should know,' she started nervously. 'Liz isn't in her room.'

'Isn't in her room?' he repeated. 'Where is she?'

'I don't know. They're looking for her at the airport.' Quickly Kate told him how Liz had gone to the airport and asked to be picked up later.

'I see,' Richard said coolly. 'So you took it upon yourself to ring the airport without telling me anything about all this.'

'Richard, you were busy with our emergency patient.

It was the middle of the night. I didn't want to worry you,' she said quickly. In the cold light of day, her reasoning seemed illogical.

'I'm in charge here,' he said angrily. 'I should have been informed. I'd better go to the airport and see if I can find her myself. If anything has happened to her, I shall hold you responsible.' His steely grey eyes were cold and hard as he glared at her. 'I think the sooner you go back to England the better.' He stormed out of the office and Kate heard a screech of tyres as he tore off down the drive.

She fought to hold back the tears, but it was no use. This was the cruellest blow of all. She could take no more. Blindly she dabbed at her eyes in a vain attempt to stem the flow of tears. Richard was right; the sooner she returned to England the better. She picked up the phone and dialled David's number. His father answered and explained that David was out on a call.

'Can I give him a message?' he asked.

The deep reassuring voice helped to calm her down. 'I've been held up by an emergency here at the nursing home, so I missed my plane. I shall be coming on a later one.'

'I see,' there was a slight pause, then Dr Murray continued. 'My dear, I know it's none of my business but I feel I must take this opportunity of giving you a little advice.'

Kate felt a moment of panic, but the gentle voice continued.

'Your mother and I had a long discussion about you and we both agreed that David has no right to insist on your returning to England. He has always taken you for granted, ever since you were small. Kate, I want you to be sure that David is the man you really want. Marriage

is for keeps you know. Don't give up your freedom out
of a sense of duty. David is young enough to find
someone else—in fact he seems quite keen on our new
nurse.' He laughed nervously. Kate did not reply.

'Are you still there?' asked Dr Murray anxiously.

'Yes, I'm here,' said Kate in a small miserable voice.
Her thoughts were in turmoil.

'Are you all right, my dear?' he asked.

'Yes, I'm all right. I'm just a little tired. I'll ring back
later when David's in. Thank you Dr Murray. You've
always been so kind. Goodbye.'

'Goodbye, my dear. Take care of yourself.'

She put the phone down. Why, oh why couldn't Dr
Murray have said this to her before? Why had he waited
until she had burned all her boats. There was no escape
now. She had tasted freedom, but it was over. She must
return to England and make the best of things. Opening
wide the windows Kate saw that the sun was rising above
the garden like a huge ball of fire. The magic of the early
morning was casting a glow over the tropical flowers. For
a few brief seconds she allowed herself to dwell on what
might have been, before she pulled herself together and
went back to the children's room.

Fiona was awake and sitting up in her bed. 'How's
Mummy?' she asked, anxiously.

'She's much better,' said Kate, smiling at the little girl.
'I'll take you to see her soon.'

Kate busied herself with the usual nursing routine,
checking on all the patients. She was pleased with the
condition of the children's mother. There were going to
be no problems there.

When Julie came on duty, Kate had finished most of
the routine work and was preparing to start the special-
ised treatment.

'Sorry I'm late,' said Julie. 'I didn't mean to leave all the work to you. How's it going?'

'Very well,' said Kate with an eagerness which she did not feel. 'Even our emergency patients are behaving themselves.'

'Good. Where's Richard?'

'He's gone to the airport to find Liz,' said Kate quietly.

'Oh, no!' Julie gasped. 'Was he annoyed?'

'No,' said Kate simply. 'He was furious. I've never seen him so angry. I think I'd better go before he gets back.'

'Please don't go just yet, Kate,' implored Julie. The ringing of the phone interrupted her. She picked it up and then handed it to Kate.

'It's Dr Clark for you,' she said.

Kate took the phone. 'Hello James. This is Kate.'

'My dear, I'm so glad you asked me to check with the agency,' he said. 'I've just heard from them; Nurse Mason has no qualifications whatsoever. She's a complete fraud.'

Kate's eyes widened.

'What is it?' said Julie anxiously.

'Ssh. I'll tell you in a minute. It's about Liz,' she whispered and then continued. 'Yes, I'm listening. But how did she fool the agency in the first place?'

'Her impeccable references were forgeries. Apparently her father is a con man, who's been in prison several times. He had assumed the identity of a millionaire, forged signatures on stolen cheques and sent his daughter out to find herself a rich husband. He was arrested at Heathrow airport this morning, trying to leave for South America.'

'Phew!' Kate breathed.

'What is it?' whispered Julie, but Kate was listening to Dr Clark.

'Under the circumstances, I think I'd better speak to Richard,' he said.

Kate paused before answering. 'I'm afraid he's not here at the moment. He's gone to the airport to look for Nurse Mason. She went there yesterday afternoon and we haven't seen her since.'

Dr Clark gave a short humourless laugh. 'Then I would imagine he's gone on a wild-goose chase. I doubt very much if we shall ever see Nurse Mason again. If she managed to get away yesterday before the police arrested her father, then she'll be miles away by now.'

'I expect so,' Kate said thoughtfully.

'I told the agency we should need a replacement as soon as possible,' he continued. 'They're sending a trained nurse out tomorrow. This time they've checked and double-checked her qualifications and references,' he added.

'I should hope so,' said Kate.

'My dear, I'm sorry you've had all this trouble. When are you coming back to England?' he asked.

'I'd better stay now until the replacement arrives. I'll give you a ring tomorrow,' she said.

'Fine, goodbye my dear.'

There was a click as he put the phone down. 'What was all that about?' asked Julie impatiently.

'As we thought,' Kate said briefly. 'Liz was a fraud—no qualifications and her father has been arrested for forgery.'

Julie gasped in amazement. 'I can't believe it. I knew she was useless, but I never guessed we should uncover something like this. Then . . .' She stopped and looked

at Kate with wide eyes. 'She's probably taken off somewhere.'

'It certainly looks like it. I must admit it had crossed
my mind last night, but I didn't want to say anything,'
said Kate.

'Poor Richard,' said Julie. 'What a shock for him.'

'Yes, poor Richard,' repeated Kate quietly. She
suddenly felt desperately tired. 'Look Julie, will you
take over for a while. I need a break; I've been here all
night.'

'Of course; I'm sorry, Kate; you should have gone off
sooner. Go and have a good rest.'

'I'll stay on until the replacement comes tomorrow,'
said Kate.

'Thanks, Kate,' Julie smiled.

Kate made her way across the garden. The sun was
now high in the sky, beating down with a ferocious
tropical glare. She hurried into her room and stripped
off her clothes. The cooling shower was soothing to
her tired, aching body and she let the water cascade
over her for several minutes. She stepped out of the
shower and wrapping herself in a large fluffy bath towel,
lay down on the bed. Then she remembered David.
Better let him know she was delayed for yet another
day. She picked up the bedside phone and dialled his
number.

'David, this is Kate,' she said, as soon as she recognised the voice at the other end. 'I'm afraid I've been
delayed yet again. I can't leave until tomorrow.'

David did not reply so she asked, 'David, are you
there? Did you hear me?'

'Yes, I heard you,' he said coolly. 'What excuse have
you got this time?'

'It's not an excuse,' she flashed back at him. 'Last

night we had an emergency, and now I have to wait for a replacement nurse to arrive.'

'Don't give me all that rubbish,' he shouted angrily. 'You can't bear to leave your new boyfriend. If that's how you feel you needn't bother to come back at all. I can manage without you.'

Kate felt suddenly very calm. The turmoil in her head had cleared and she was in control of the situation at last. She spoke evenly and concisely. 'I'm glad you don't need me any more, David,' she said. It was if a large weight had been removed from her shoulders.

'Answer me one question,' snarled David. 'Do you love him?'

Kate paused and took in a deep breath before replying, 'Oh yes, I love him. I love him very much.'

The phone went dead; Kate sat very still before she replaced the receiver. As she did so she was aware of a slight movement by the door. Looking up she saw Richard standing there.

'I'm sorry,' he said quietly. 'I did knock but there was no reply. I didn't mean to startle you. I came to tell you about Liz.'

'Have you been waiting long?' asked Kate.

'Long enough,' he said softly as he crossed the room.

Kate was suddenly aware that she was covered only in a bath towel. She looked around anxiously for her robe. Richard smiled at her confusion, and tossed it on to the bed for her.

'Here, put this on if it makes you feel happier,' he grinned. 'I won't watch.'

Kate struggled into the robe, and then Richard turned impatiently to face her.

'Kate, I couldn't help overhearing you on the phone just now. Who are you in love with? Is it Mike?'

'No, of course not . . . Oh Richard.' Nothing could prevent the tears from flowing down her cheeks. Richard took her in his arms and covered her face with kisses.

'My darling, oh my darling,' he murmured. 'I love you so much.'

'And I love you, Richard,' she breathed.

He kissed her passionately, pausing only to ask, 'Kate, will you marry me?'

'Yes, oh yes I will, Richard.'

His hot kisses rained down upon her and she was lost in the ecstasy of his embrace.

Some time later as she lay in Richard's arms Kate asked innocently, 'Did you find Liz at the airport?'

'No, it was very odd. I checked the passenger lists and apparently she flew out yesterday,' said Richard.

'To South America?' asked Kate quietly.

'Yes. How did you know?'

'I'll tell you later. It's not important now. Are you sad she's gone?'

'Sad? I'm delighted! She was really becoming too much to handle. I was counting the days to the end of her contract. I used to flirt with her in the hope that I might make you jealous, as you made me jealous with Mike.'

'Mike never meant anything to me. He was just a good friend.' She moved in Richard's arms and he kissed her slowly, savouring the taste of her lips.

'I've always loved you, Kate,' he murmured. 'Ever since I saw you at the airport. At first I didn't dare to love again. It was too soon. Then when I thought you loved your fiancé, I felt I had no right to break up your engagement. I had to force myself to criticise you so that you wouldn't see I was in love with you. But at the back of my mind there was always a slight hope that one day you might be mine. That was why I bought Ogiwa House.'

'Oh, Richard. I'd forgotten about that. How marvellous!' she breathed.

'I felt I had to have it,' he continued, 'because it was part of your life. I would always know that you had lived there. Now we can live there together when we're married. We'll have our own family.'

'It's a wonderful place for children,' said Kate happily.

'Kate, oh Kate, I can't believe we're together at last,' breathed Richard. 'I want to hold you in my arms forever.'

Kate lay back on the bed, gazing up at the strong handsome man who was soon to be her husband. His hands caressed her body beneath the thin silky robe. She felt an uncontrollable surge of desire as he held her close.

He kissed her mouth hungrily, as his impatient hands opened her robe. 'I think we should get married as soon as possible,' he murmured, as he held her trembling body. 'I don't think either of us can hold out much longer. How about next week?'

Kate laughed in delight and pushed him away with mock modesty. 'I can be ready if you can,' she said. 'Oh, I nearly forgot. How did you get on at Kyruba Hospital?'

'I've got the job,' he said quietly. 'I'm the new medical consultant.'

'Congratulations, darling.' Kate kissed him softly. 'But then I always thought you'd get it. My father used to say, "May the best man win", and I knew you were the best man for the job . . . the best man for me . . . the only man I have ever loved.'

'And I shall love you forever,' murmured Richard, as his lips closed once more on hers, sealing their eternal love.

Doctor Nurse Romances

Romance in the wide world of medicine

Amongst the intense emotional pressures of modern medical life, doctors and nurses often find romance. Read about their lives and loves in the other two Doctor Nurse titles available this month.

FLYAWAY SISTER
by Lisa Cooper

Casualty Sister Dawn Campion is strangely reluctant to volunteer her help for the newly-formed Isle of Wight air-ambulance service. After this inauspicious start to her working relationship with the dynamic Dr Miles Stratton, how can she possibly survive the proximity inevitable in such vital work?

LADY IN HARLEY STREET
by Anne Vinton

It seems the answer to Dr Celia Derwent's prayers when her new boss Dr Alan Grainger proposes marriage. She desperately needs a husband in order to convince the courts that she should have custody of her orphaned niece Fiona, and Alan is devoted to Fiona. But will this marriage of convenience really solve all Celia's problems?

Mills & Boon
the rose of romance

 **ROMANCE**

Variety is the spice of romance

Each month, Mills & Boon publish new romances. New stories about people falling in love. A world of variety in romance – from the best writers in the romantic world. Choose from these titles in March.

LORD OF THE LAND Margaret Rome
CALL UP THE STORM Jane Donnelly
BETRAYAL Charlotte Lamb
THE DEVIL'S ADVOCATE Vanessa James
VISION OF LOVE Elizabeth Graham
CHAINS OF GOLD Yvonne Whittal
CLOUDED RAPTURE Margaret Pargeter
THE FLAWED MARRIAGE Penny Jordan
MIDSUMMER STAR Betty Neels
LOVE'S ONLY DECEPTION Carole Mortimer
PASSIONATE ENEMIES Kathryn Cranmer
SEA LIGHTNING Linda Harrel

On sale where you buy paperbacks. If you require further information or have any difficulty obtaining them, write to: Mills & Boon Reader Service, PO Box 236, Thornton Road, Croydon, Surrey CR9 3RU, England.

Mills & Boon
the rose of romance

How to join in a whole new world of romance

It's very easy to subscribe to the Mills & Boon Reader Service. As a regular reader, you can enjoy a whole range of special benefits. Bargain offers. Big cash savings. Your own free Reader Service newsletter, packed with knitting patterns, recipes, competitions, and exclusive book offers.

We send you the very latest titles each month, postage and packing free – no hidden extra charges. There's absolutely no commitment – you receive books for only as long as you want.

We'll send you details. Simply send the coupon – or drop us a line for details about the Mills & Boon Reader Service Subscription Scheme. Post to: Mills & Boon Reader Service, P.O. Box 236, Thornton Road, Croydon, Surrey CR9 3RU, England. *Please note: READERS IN SOUTH AFRICA please write to: Mills & Boon Reader Service of Southern Africa, Private Bag X3010, Randburg 2125, S. Africa.

Please send me details of the Mills & Boon Subscription Scheme.

NAME (Mrs/Miss) _____ EP3

ADDRESS _____

_____

COUNTY/COUNTRY _____ POST/ZIP CODE _____

BLOCK LETTERS, PLEASE

Mills & Boon
the rose of romance